THE WHEEL OF FATE

TWISTED BY TAROT

BOOK ONE

MIA ELLIOT

The Wheel of Fate

Contents

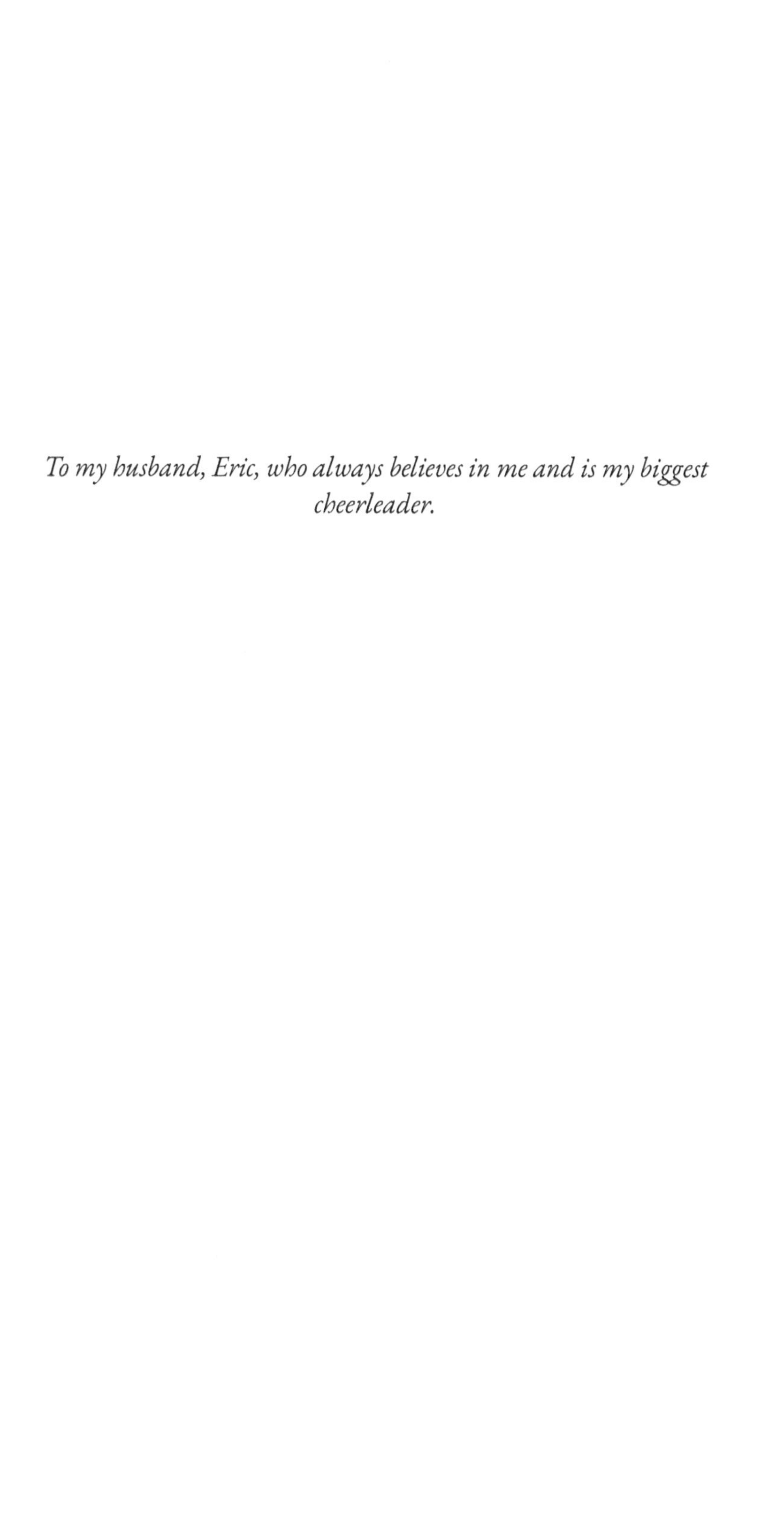

*To my husband, Eric, who always believes in me and is my biggest
cheerleader.*

The Wheel of Fate
Mia Elliot

A fate twisted by tarot ...

There's nothing Knox Roffe wants more than to find his mate, not even becoming Alpha. He's scoured every wolf pack, but still hasn't found her. He's desperate, and when he learns of a witch who just might have the power to locate her, he can't say no ... no matter the cost.

Bailey Dennis doesn't need a man in her life. She just got out of a toxic relationship, and she's got enough going on with trying to figure herself out. Still, she's about to watch her best friend get married, and part of her is a tad envious.

Can the Witch of Bonds bring a shifter looking for love and a human scared to get hurt again together ... or will her tarot cards leave the two with broken hearts in a tangled fate?

The Wheel of Fate is Book 1 in the *Twisted by Tarot* series, a collection of spicy novellas featuring the Witch of Bonds and her soulmate magic!

ONE

The air is heavy with sandalwood and certainty. Plants and various crystals hang from every corner, bits of light bouncing off them and sprinkling the room in shards of light. Candles litter every shelf, their still flames casting shadows amongst every nook and cranny of the crowded back room. Past a beaded curtain too bland for the space, I look at the small table in the center of the floor. On it sits a large deck of cards, each stacked face down with black, purple, and gold symbols adorning their backsides.

"Sit," the witch instructs, taking a seat in the plusher of the two chairs. I glance around nervously, wondering if this was a good idea.

"I'm not sure—"

"You're in the right place," she assures me, as though she can read my mind. "No one comes to me who isn't meant to."

"Ever?" I ask, but she shoots me an exasperated look as she shuffles the deck of cards.

"Sit," she says again, and I pull out the seat across from her. She watches me intently as she shuffles, the corners of her mouth curling up slightly. I'm not sure how old she is. One can never quite tell with witches. The slight wrinkles around her mouth and between her brows tell me she's not as young as she once was, but she could easily be in her hundreds and using magic to appear in her forties.

"So, you're tired of waiting?" she says.

"I'm sorry?"

"That's why you're here. You're looking for your one true mate, and you think that I can help you find her. Or him."

"I don't care who my mate is. I just don't want to be alone anymore. They're surely a shifter, but I've been through all the wolf packs in the area and have yet to find her."

"Perhaps she's not a shifter at all," the witch says.

"But ... we always mate within our kind," I say.

She smiles wickedly. "We'll see." She sets the cards down and holds out a hand. Past crimson nails, I notice a rat tattoo that travels up her wrist and disappears into her sleeve. "Agatha Nicholson, but you've probably heard me called the Witch of Bonds. At least, rumor on the street is that's what they call me these days."

"These days?" I ask, but she simply cocks a brow and smiles. I clear my throat, placing my hand in hers.

She gives it a firm shake, then waves her arm over the top of the table. "The cards can help find your mate, but know this: Magic always comes at a price."

"What sort of price?"

She smiles, refusing to elaborate. "I am not a god, I can't create something from nothing, and you shouldn't expect this. If you do—"

"I don't," I assure her, "but I don't want to wait any longer. I don't want to be alone anymore. Every day that passes where I stay unmated leaves me more miserable. I can't take it anymore. I need to find her. I don't care what it costs. Whatever it is, it'll be worth it."

"If you're sure," she says. With a flourish, she spreads the deck of cards across the tabletop, fanning them out until they all lay visible. She runs her hands above the cards, her palms hovering mere inches from them as she hums and haws. "Hmmm. Yes. The cards feel very alive today, buzzing with energy. I think they'll do well for you, Knox Roffe."

"How do you—"

She waves a dismissive hand. "The cards can tell a great many things to those who really listen. And if you want this to work, Knox, then you'll have to really listen."

"How do I know which card to pick?"

"Let your hands linger," she instructs. "Feel their energy. Take your time. The right card will call out to you, as will your mate once the cards have decided your fate."

I nod, exhaling deeply as I look over the cards. "Okay. Here goes nothing." I do as she says, letting my hand hover over the cards. One by one, I pass them by, not feeling anything, not hearing anything but my labored breathing as my hand trembles, nervously panning the table. I'm nearly at the last card in the row when I feel it. It starts as a buzzing in my palm, then travels up my wrist until my whole arm tingles menacingly. I pick up the card, ignoring the biting prickles as I touch it.

"Set it here," Agatha says, waving to a spot on the table near her. I place it face-up, and she gasps.

"What?" I ask, heart beating in my chest. "Is it bad?"

"None of the cards are *bad*," she harps. "It all depends on what you do with them. This one that's called to you, The Wheel. It signifies change, cycles, and an inevitable fate."

"That's good, right? I bet the change will be the inevitable fate of my mate and I finding each other. And the cycles must mean the end of my cycle of loneliness. That all makes sense."

"The cards are rarely as simple and straightforward as they initially seem," she muses, picking the card up and looking at it a long while before setting it down in front of me. The embossed gold wheel shimmers and dances with the now-flickering flames in the dimly lit room.

I run my fingers over the card. The strange buzzing I felt when I initially touched it has gone. No matter how long I stare at it, it seems nothing more than an ordinary card. "I don't feel any different. Aren't I supposed to feel something?"

Agatha smiles, her top lip curling up in a sneer. "I haven't sealed your reading with a spell yet, dear. But I must ask one last time: Are you sure you want to do this?"

I take a deep breath, my stomach clenching in a thousand knots. "I'm sure. I'll do anything to find her. Sacrifice anything so long as you can guarantee this will work."

"Oh, it'll work alright. When I'm done, I will begin to sense your fated love. The cards will lead me to her. Once I'm sure it's her, I'll cast a spell that will signal you to her location. You'll feel a strong pull, an inescapable desire to move to her. But you must be patient. Are you ready?"

"I am," I say confidently.

Agatha waves her hands around each other, and a ball of light blue smoke forms. I stare in disbelief as the tattoo on her hand transforms into a live rat, crawling into the palm of her hand and hissing loudly as the blue cloud floats all around, the smoke surrounding me until I can barely see across the table.

I cough loudly, fanning the smoke from my face as Agatha whispers indiscernibly. A piercing sound fills the room as I shut my eyes and cover my ears. My head is spinning, and for a moment, I feel as though I might pass out.

Then, as quickly as they started, the noise and smoke dissipate. I open my eyes slowly, the rat and cards having vanished. There's nothing here but Agatha and her witchy room, the candles all having grown still again.

"You can go now," she says firmly, again flicking a dismissive hand in my direction. "The spell will work. The tarot has confirmed it will be done."

I look around the room. I don't know what I expected, but I feel no different. "So ... that's it? Just like that? That's all I needed?"

Agatha sighs. "You ask too many questions. Go, go back to your routine. The magic will lead me to your mate; you'll know when I've found her. As as soon as you feel a pull, head in that direction. You'll know it's her when you lay eyes on her."

I nod, nothing left to say to the mysterious woman. As I step out into the low light of the evening, Agatha calls out from behind me. I turn and see her standing there, an ear-to-ear grin suiting the mischievous twinkle in her dark eyes.

"May she love you in all your forms, Knox," she says. I bolt out of there, not daring to look back again.

Two

Bailey

TWO MONTHS LATER

I look around, admiring my handiwork. I may have gone a little overboard on the decorations and snacks. The pink and purple ribbons are giving 'girls' night.' Hosting Cassie's bachelorette party may mean a lot of cleanup afterward, but it's the least I can do for my best friend right before she gets married to the love of her life.

I sigh gently. Cassie lucked out when she met Troy backpacking across Europe three years ago. They couldn't be more perfect together, and he's a great guy. And here I am, alone, having just escaped the shittiest relationship of my life. I spent nearly two years with a narcissistic pig who I recently discovered was cheating on me every single time he went out of town for a work function.

What. A. Douchebag.

I push thoughts of Zach from my mind as I finish setting out the trays of fruits and veggies I cut earlier. Everything is in order, just in time, as a loud knock on the door signals Cassie's arrival. She doesn't wait for me to open it, barging in with a small suitcase and several reusable grocery bags in tow.

"Oh my gosh, Bay! Look at this place! You did all this by your-self? How did you even hang those that high?" She shoves the door closed with a hip and kicks her shoes off before waltzing over to the kitchen island and setting all her bags down.

"I've got a ladder in the shed out back. You're cutting it pretty close, aren't you? Everyone else is supposed to be here—"

"I'll get it!" Cassie yells as someone rings the bell, bounding across the open room. I envy how happy and carefree she always looks, squealing excitedly as all of our girlfriends start showing up.

The night is in full swing within the hour. Everyone arrived safely despite my cabin being in a tricky, rural location. Drinks have been had, snacks intermittently enjoyed, and it's almost time for the surprise event I booked for Cassie. I grin wildly when the doorbell rings, and Cassie shoots me a curious look.

"Tell me those are male strippers," she says, expression deadpan.

I roll my eyes. "Please. First, I wasn't about to ask Troy how he'd feel about that. Secondly, you actually think I can afford that on my salary as a grocery store clerk? I wish."

"Who is it then?" She demands.

"You'll seeeee," I coo, the warm buzz of alcohol flowing through my words. I sprint to the door and open it to see a middle-aged woman standing there. She's pretty, with red lipstick and a purple cloak that looks like something out of a movie.

"Hello, dear. You must be Bailey," she says, holding out a tattooed hand which I happily shake.

"Hey! Yes, come in!" I close the door behind her. "You find the place okay?"

"I knew exactly where I needed to go," she says cryptically.

"Cool!" Cassie gushes, jumping up from the couch to greet the tarot reader. "Who are you?"

"Agatha Nicholson, dear. Bailey hired me to do a tarot read-ing. She says you're getting married."

"I am! Aww, Bailey! You didn't tell me you hired a psychic!"

"I'm not a psychic," Agatha says flatly. She heads over to the living area and sits on the rug at one end of the coffee table. The rest of the girls look on curiously as Cassie and I join them. "Is here alright?" Agatha asks.

"Sure," I say. "Cassie, do you wanna—"

"Why don't I do a reading for you first?" Agatha says.

"Well, I thought Cassie—"

"Please," Agatha interjects, "I insist. It's tradition for the person who contacted the reader to go first. The person who reached out often needs a reading most of all, regardless of the reason for contacting me."

I look at Cassie, and she shrugs. "Go for it, Bailey," she says.

"Alright," I agree, taking a seat.

Agatha pulls a black velvet bag from an inner pocket on her cloak, opening its drawstring and pulling out the deck of cards within. She begins shuffling the deck, her eyes locked on mine. "Now, I want you to think about what's missing from your life, dear. What do you desire? What would complete it?"

"I—"

"Shh, don't tell us!" Agatha cries, and the rest of the ladies giggle. "Just ... think about it. Picture it. What do you lack?"

My bruised heart can't help picturing the last good memory I have of Zach and me together before I discovered the lies and betrayal. The two of us went to Hawaii six months ago. It seemed perfect then, except my naive-ass was disappointed he didn't propose to me.

In hindsight? Thank god.

Agatha fans the cards across the table, their backs beautifully decorated with ornate symbols. "Choose," she says firmly.

I look at the row of cards, debating whether to pick from an end or more central. I go to grab one from the left but can't ignore the pull that sends my hand right to the second-last card. I flip it over and set it in front of me, admiring the gold-embossed picture of an upside-down wheel.

Agatha's smile is so wide I can see her unnaturally white teeth. "I knew it," she hisses under her breath.

"Excuse me?" I say, unable to stifle a giggle. "Is this rigged?"

The look on Agatha's face has me shrinking back, her eyes alight with a glimmer of madness in her offense. "You don't rig tarot, Miss Dennis. And the cards don't lie. Ever."

I clear my throat, glancing at Cassie and the other girls as they stare awkwardly. The room has grown uncomfortably silent, the air stuffy with tension. "Okay, so what does this card mean?"

Agatha's solemn look rattles me. "The wheel signifies change and an inevitable fate … but you've pulled it in reverse."

"Okay." I stare at the card, refusing to let the piece of glorified cardboard wig me out. "And what does *that* mean?"

"It represents a lack of control. Trying to cling to control. The card tells you that change is coming your way, and you must be willing to sacrifice some control and allow things to come to you." She places a hand on the card, nodding knowingly as she hums. "Yes, I see a fated mate coming your way. A shifter. Someone you very strongly need to be open to."

Cassie bursts out laughing. "What? A shifter? You mean like a werewolf? That's ridiculous. Where did you find this woman, Bailey?"

Agatha scoops all the cards off the table with an inhumanly expeditious swipe. "I can't help those that aren't open to the tarot's teachings. Good luck with the wedding, Ms. Hewitt." She bags the cards and returns them to their spot in her pocket, then turns to me with narrowed eyes as she stands. "I suggest you become much more open to possibilities, Miss Dennis, lest you scramble the fate the tarot has in place for you and find yourself in a bad predicament." And with that, she storms out, slamming the door behind her.

The girls and I sit in shock for a moment. Then, the entire gang bursts into giggles.

"What a weirdo!" Cassie cries. "Seriously, Bay, where did you find her?"

I shrug. "I saw an ad online; I thought it sounded cool! I'm sorry, Cass. You didn't even get to do a reading."

"That's okay," she says, strolling into the kitchen. "But that was weird. I need another drink. Anyone else?"

A loud cheer erupts, and the rest of the girls join her to mix fresh drinks.

I down the rest of my cup, sad the tarot experience didn't go better ... and wondering how Agatha knew Cass's last name when I'm sure I didn't include it in our emails.

THREE

KNOX

The unquenchable thirst that leaves you raw and desperate on a scorching summer day hits me hard. The pull towards her is like nothing I've ever felt before. Agatha told me there'd be a sudden aching I couldn't ignore, but is this the price she warned I'd have to pay? A longing so intense it's damn near suffocating?

I gulp down air, but it isn't enough. I look down at the half-finished cabinet I was building and scoff. There's no way I can finish my work now, not today. The overwhelming ache to head north is turning into a screaming agony. My legs feel on fire with how badly I need to move. I can't stay in my workshop a second longer. I need to see her.

But first, I must call Agatha to ensure this is the real deal.

She never confirmed whether she found my fated mate; she just said I would know when she did. And this pull may be telling me to head north, but I don't want to take off blindly running until I hear it from the witch's mouth.

She picks up before the phone even has the chance to ring. "It's time, Knox."

"This is really it, then? You mean it? This is—"

"Yes. Your fated mate has been summoned. The tarot has

done as promised. And, as you promised, you must pay your dues."

"I'm paying them right now, witch. My skin feels like it's on fire. I can't think, I can't concentrate, I can't—"

"How you feel is irrelevant," she snaps coldly. "Go to your mate. Go in the direction that's calling to you. You'll know her when you see, and when you do ... all will be revealed."

"What's that supposed to mean?" I ask, but glancing at my phone shows the call's been disconnected. "Shit," I mumble. Agatha's vague statement aside, the burning in my legs continues to grow. It's now clawing its way up my hips and torso, and I'm afraid I'll soon combust if I don't get a move on.

I shift into my wolf form, taking off on all fours to cover ground quickly. It takes me over an hour to get to the city limits, away from my little cabin in the countryside just south of the city. I run all night, opting to run along the outer west edge rather than straight through. A wolf is an unwanted trespasser in rural spots; The city is a goddamn death sentence.

My journey leads me around the city's outskirts and out the northwest corner, my furiously burning legs carrying me straight through the night. A vibrant full moon hangs above me, lighting the way to a quaint tiny home nestled on a small plot of farmland. It seems she also lives in the middle of nowhere, an endearing fact I doubt is coincidental.

I creep up to the property, paws pressing into the grass with stealthy silence. I shove my nose over the edge of the window and see her: A beautiful woman with long, dark hair and a curvy frame facing away from me. She's dancing to classical music while flipping something in a pan, her hips swaying rhythmically with the beat. The open window wafts the smell of fried eggs my way, but more potent than that is a scent that draws me in and makes it impossible to look away.

Her distinctly human scent hits me, her very essence flooding my nostrils and filling me with an intoxicating mixture of need and serenity.

This is her—my fated mate.

Agatha was right; she isn't a shifter at all. This is going to complicate things. Shifters aren't out to the rest of the world, especially not to humans.

As she turns to grab a plate from a cupboard, my eyes take in every minute detail of her face. Long bangs sweep across her forehead, messily falling over one eye as she stretches up to reach the plates. Round cheeks and a slender nose lead to a set of beautiful, pouty lips, lips that I desperately long to know the taste and feel of. She spins on her heel and plates her food. Judging by the hour, I'd say she's an early bird, and this is breakfast.

She takes the plate and sits at the dining table past the kitchen, the low light of the room making her difficult to see. I risk her spotting me in human form to get a better look at her. I close my eyes and breathe, waiting for that familiar sensation of my body changing, but nothing comes. No matter how hard I focus, nothing. I can feel my willingness to change, but it's as though a magical ward is stopping me.

Panic grips me as I realize I'm stuck in my wolf form, unable to shift.

Unable to show that dazzling creature my true self, the self she's bound to fall in love with.

I watch her a bit longer despite my inner chaos. Something about her soothes me, even in wolf form. She has an aura that's equal parts spicy and energetic as it is tranquil and calming. I want to get to know her so severely, ask her where she's from, what sorts of movies she likes, and what her hopes and dreams are so I can fulfill them all, but I've no way to ask her anything.

I have to force Agatha to change me back.

I fight the urge to stay outside my mate's window. It's hard to ignore the tether between us as I turn and run the opposite way, but I need this dealt with sooner rather than later. My mate is never going to be able to accept me like this. Not when she's a human, and I'm ... *this*.

I run so hard to Agatha's that my legs throb when I get there.

Her little brick house is in a sparsely populated neighborhood with more shops and laundromats than actual housing, and I realize it is not too far from my mate's house. I get to her place, and she opens the door wide, not bothering to invite me in. The sun is barely beginning to peek over the horizon, most humans still fast asleep in their beds.

"I knew you'd come," she says, but I growl loudly in response, baring my teeth to show her I mean business.

All she does is laugh, a cackle that sounds all the more horrendous this hour of day.

"Patience, wolf," she says, spitting the sour words in my direction. "I need you to be patient and have faith in the deck. The tarot will seal the fate of you and your mate together, but you have to give it time. And I did warn you there'd be a price. You've sacrificed some magic, the magic to shift, it seems, temporarily. Consider it an offering to the deck and all the power it holds. Nothing lasts forever, but for now ... you'll have to stay like this."

I growl again, but she gives me a no-nonsense look that has my tail subconsciously tucking between my legs. If she isn't going to help me, then there's only one thing left to do.

I have to convince the love of my life to fall in love with this side of me.

FOUR

BAILEY

I can't believe it.

I've looked goddamn everywhere, and I can't find them. They're not in my purse, on the coffee table, or the kitchen island. I even checked my jacket pockets, and I've yet to find my keys anywhere. And if I don't see them quickly, this will be the fourth time I'll have been late to work the past two months. I usually have my shit way more together than this, but after that lousy breakup with Zach, I've been in a weird headspace that's made it hard to keep track of things.

As if that loser didn't ruin my life enough by humiliating me, my ex-coworker filled me in about all of his illicit affairs, including her.

I look in my purse again. There is nothing in there but a couple of maxed-out credit cards and a smattering of grocery receipts.

Fuck.

Typical Monday, things going awry before the day has even officially started. I search the kitchen again, moving the fruit dish and coffee maker out of the way to check every nook and cranny. Nothing.

The back of my neck prickles when I hear a sound coming

from outside. I step cautiously over to the nearest window and pull the curtain back, looking out over the little wooden deck attached to the front of my cabin. I don't see anything, but then I hear it again—the distinct sound of something knocking up against the door.

I feel almost nauseous as I head toward the door. Considering how far outside the city I live, there'd never be anyone randomly popping by. And Cassie may know the way here so well that she could drive it with her eyes closed, but she'd never pop in on me with no warning, especially not on a Monday morning.

I check my phone, noting the couple of bars of cell reception. At least, if there is a murderer outside my door, I can call the cops right before I get killed. The likelihood of someone making it out of these woods without getting caught is next to nil.

Grasping my phone tightly, I unlock my front door and open it slowly. It creaks open, early-morning sunlight pouring onto my floor in a wide streak as I squint against the light.

No one. Nothing here.

I look around. I was sure I heard someone tapping on my door slightly, but now I'm not sure. Having concluded I must be going crazy, I shut it quickly and am stopped by a familiar jingling sound.

My keys.

I look down at the lock, and my keys are just hanging there. I clearly must have been extra tired when I got home last night. I never leave my keys in the door, yet here they are. I sigh in exasperation as I grab them and run inside, stepping into my shoes and beelining across the room to retrieve my purse and coat from where I left them on the sofa.

I head out and lock the door behind me. I turn around, fully intending to leap off the deck and see a creature standing there.

And not just any creature, but the most enormous damn wolf I've ever seen.

It stands at over half my height on all fours. I stifle a scream as I drop my purse and keys. My bottom lip trembles as I try to formulate words. "Nice ... Nice wolf. Good wolf. That's a good boy."

I grab the doorknob behind me and give it a couple of good shakes, but it's still locked. I knew it would be, yet somehow my brain was praying it wouldn't. I stare at the wolf, intimidated by its sheer size and the solemnness of its gray eyes. It watches me, its head cocking as I slowly bend down and tap around on the deck in search of my keys. I don't dare take my eyes off the wolf.

Or, more accurately, I *can't*.

Words can't explain it, but I feel this incredible pull to the creature. Its eyes are stormy skies, dark and vast as they hold my gaze. Its brown fur is highlighted by a reddish glow in the morning light. I take a deep breath as my fingertips kiss the coolness of metal, my hand snapping around my keys and yanking them into my chest.

Still, the wolf watches.

"That's a good boy," I coo, standing as slowly as I crouched. "Gooood boy. I'm just gonna put these keys in my door now, okay?"

I glance down at the lock, fumbling the keys around, searching for the keyhole. Peeling my eyes from the wolf feels like a mountainous effort. It's as though the longer it watches me, the more I want it to.

Surely, this is just my body's strange reaction to terror.

I feel the key slip in and gasp in relief, but it's short-lived as the wolf approaches me. I try to get the key to turn, but the angle of my hand makes it finicky, and I can't quite get it open. I crouch down again to grab my purse and get more leverage, but it's the wrong move.

The wolf bounds up onto the deck, a shrill scream emitting from me and scaring all the birds from neighboring trees. I feel sick to my stomach as the creature plants itself in front of me, my body crouched down and huddled against the door. It comes up to me, its breath hot on my face as I pinch my eyes shut and wait for whatever awful fate is in store.

The feel of something wet and hot scrapes from my chin to my cheek, and I open my eyes with trembling breath. It's sitting in front of me, its gray eyes having gone big and puppy-like. It licks my cheek again, and I smile. From this angle, the creature is very clearly male.

"Oh," I say softly. "That's ... not at all what I was expecting. I thought you were gonna eat my face off!"

The wolf whines, forcing his head up against my chest until I start petting him. He nuzzles into my neck as I scratch behind one of his ears. It's strange, but something about him feels safe and familiar, like coffee with an old friend you didn't realize you'd missed so much.

Like ... Like we're meeting for the thousandth time.

I continue petting his head a second longer, then realize I'm still running late for work.

"Shit! I'm sorry, wolf, I've got to go! I'm late for work!"

I gather up my purse and lock my door again, then dash to my car. When I look back, the wolf is still sitting on my deck.

Just ... sitting there.

FIVE

KNOX

The taste of her skin on my tongue is liquid fire. I want to have more of her.

I *need* to have more of her.

And thanks to the fucking Witch of Bonds and her crazy tarot deck, I can't even let my mate see the real me. The me she's supposed to be falling in love with. The me that should be sheltering her from the world in strong, human arms.

The me that should be making love to her in the moonlight.

A flicker of sadness courses through me at the thought, but it's quickly replaced by one of rage. Was this the only way to find my way to her? Black magic sorcery and an imprisonment that will last god knows how long?

I watch my raven-haired goddess throw her keys into the ignition and take off down the gravel pathway leading to the highway. I can't even ask her her name in this state, nor tell her mine. And while she may not see me as a viable mate right now, that doesn't mean I can't keep close to her and ensure she stays safe.

I leap off the deck and take off running, wearing the trees alongside the highway as a disguise. I follow her car, running beside her for her forty-minute commute to the central city. I crouch here and duck there to keep her from seeing me and keep as hidden as possible from other humans. I watch her get ready in her car, throwing mascara on in the rearview and putting a little red vest over her top. When she steps inside, it dawns on me.

Ah, so this is where she works.

She's honestly the only ray of sunshine in the godforsaken place. Zombies stand at all the other registers, humans with dark bags and hollow cheeks and no life zest left in them. But she stands at one of the registers wearing a smile that radiates warmth throughout the space, and more customers come to her than anyone else.

I stay there for her whole shift, watching her. She's got this buzz to her, this energetic bounce in her step that's electrifying. I long to hold her, to know what her soft curves would feel like, wrapped tightly in my arms as she's pressed against me.

Even in my wolf state, being near her awakens my body in ways I've never experienced.

The sky turns hues of orange and crimson by the time she's off work. Her legs must scream after working a double, but nothing on her face gives it away if that's true. She's still smiling, waving goodbye to coworkers as they head out. After a bit, she's the only one left, finishing her cash out and gathering her purse before she comes out and locks up the store.

The sun bids farewell, dipping below the horizon and blanketing the city in darkness. The street lamps cast bits of light down over the sidewalk as she walks, her swaying hips causing me to salivate. She's halfway to her car when I hear thudding footsteps against concrete. It's too far for her to notice, though she stops and glances around anxiously before walking.

She senses something is wrong.

I watch as a burly man steps out from a distant alleyway. His eyes are locked on her, watching her every move. He licks his lips and picks up his pace toward her. I make my way around the far edge of the parking lot. I position myself behind my mate in some bushes outlining the parking lot, ready to intervene if necessary. No way this creep is getting anywhere near my woman.

She turns and sees the man, the light of the lamps highlighting her widening eyes. She looks scared but keeps walking confidently toward her car. She's nearly there when the man starts closing in, his dirty work boots dragging along as he takes staggering steps. The smell of alcohol pierces the air as he speaks, his swaying stature giving way to his intoxication.

"Look at you," he hisses. "Aren't you a pretty thing?"

"I ... I'm going to call the cops!" she says, but she isn't holding her phone. She reaches into her bag, but the man takes a step closer.

"Leave it, bitch."

She freezes, hand hovering above her purse. Her chest is rising and falling with panicked breaths, a sight that lights my every nerve ending on fire.

The man takes another step, damn near close enough to grab her, and it's one too many. I jump out from the bushes and rush over, the man stumbling backward and landing hard on the concrete as I growl menacingly.

He tries to stand up but falls again, using his arms to scoot himself away as fast as possible. My fangs are bared as I step in front of my mate. I can hear her trembling behind me, but she's safe now.

Whether she knows it or not, she's always safe with me.

The man climbs to his feet and takes off, tripping a couple more times and barely catching himself. He looks back and heads back into the alley from which he appeared. I watch until I'm sure he's truly gone, then turn around and face my poor, terrified mate.

Her brows raise when she looks at me, her delicate features awash with relief.

"You!" she cries, stepping closer to me. "You're the ... the wolf from my place! How ... Did you follow me here?"

I walk over to her, and she crouches down and rubs between my ears. I lick her face, the taste of her sweet to my senses. She giggles as she stares at me. "You crazy thing! I can't believe you followed me here. Thank god, though. You scared that creep away. Thank you." I nuzzle my face into her chest.

I wish I could tell her how she never has to worry anymore, how she'll always be safe now that she's my mate.

How I love her.

"I'm going to call you ... Wolfgang, okay? Actually, Wolfie. You can get in the back seat of my car, and I'll take you back to the woods. It isn't safe for you in the city."

I whine my agreement, and she smiles. She unlocks her car and opens the back door, stepping aside so I can hop in. I lay down on the seat, barely enough room to be comfortable. It likely would have been faster to head back on foot, but I won't turn down any moment I can spend with her.

We hit the road, and she puts on some quiet music, something mellow and instrumental. Not really what I would have pegged her for, but maybe it's what she likes to decompress at day's end. I lay my head on my paws and close my eyes, enjoying how her scent fills the small space.

"Seriously, Wolfie, I was really lucky back there," she says. "Lucky you followed me. Still not sure why you did that, but ... thank you. You can't keep following me to work, though. If someone sees you, it could mean big trouble."

I sense her eyes on me as she glances over her shoulder and then back at the road. "I'm Bailey, by the way. I wonder how long you've lived in those woods outside my house. How long have you —Jesus Christ, I think I'm losing my mind. Talking to a damn wolf like it's going to answer me. Yeesh. I need to get to bed."

I open my eyes and look at her in the rearview mirror. She's so beautiful. Perfect, really.

"Anyway, I'm thankful for you, is what I'm trying to say. Crazy Wolfie."

She doesn't say anything else the rest of the drive and doesn't need to.

All that matters is that she's safe.

Six

Bailey

I get in my car and head home, having parked closer to the doors. After last night, I don't think I'll ever park that far from the grocer's entrance again. It was lucky that that wolf followed me to work and scared that man off, though I've still no idea why he did that, or why he followed me in the first place.

It's weird; I don't recall ever reading anything that said it's normal wolf behavior for them to grow attached to a random human. Then again, I don't know if it's normal for a human to feel as connected to a random animal as I do to Wolfie. I can't explain it, but something about his gray eyes pulls me in and makes me feel safe and protected. As if I know he's always going to be there for me.

But that's ridiculous. He's a wild animal.

He was probably drawn to my cabin by the smell of food. The fact that he followed me to the city ... Well, who knows what the hell that was about. Maybe he's not had much luck finding food in the woods and hopes I'll feed him. Yeah, that's probably it.

I feel the familiar rumble of gravel beneath the tires as I turn down the long road that leads to my place. My heart jumps as I pull up to the deck.

There, in the soft glow of the porch light, sits Wolfie.

I get out and walk over, intrigued by how he waits patiently. "Hey, boy. You didn't sit out here all day, did you?"

I crouch down beside him, and he whines, pressing his head into my chest as I scratch behind one of his ears. His body is warm as he leans against me, and some little piece of me feels guilty at the thought of leaving him out here all alone.

But he's a wild animal. I can't have him inside. Besides, he must have a den, cave, or something he lives in. I don't know where wolves usually live, but he came from somewhere. Somewhere he needs to get back to.

I pat his head. "I have to head inside now. You should go home, okay? Go back to your pack or ... whatever. There must be somewhere you belong."

The funny thing is that some part deep inside me, some bit too loud to ignore, feels like he belongs here.

With me.

I shake it off as I head inside, glancing back. "Goodnight, Wolfie,' I say as I shut the door.

I make myself dinner while light instrumental music plays in the background. It soothes me, the melody coaxing me here and there as I float around the kitchen and sway to the beat. I glance out the window occasionally, and every time, I see Wolfie still sitting there, looking back at me.

He's still there by the time I head to bed, though he's curled up and appears to be sleeping. The porch light has gone off with the lack of movement, and only a bit of moonlight filtering through the trees gives way to his shaggy presence. The evening darkness dulls the bits of red in his fur, but the sheer size of his enormous stature is still apparent. No wonder the man in the parking lot was so quick to run away.

I shut the lights off and retire to my room, plugging my phone in and giving my face a quick wash before tucking into bed.

That night, my brain is a swarm of light and color. Vibrant

green hues glow in the sunlight of an unnaturally bright forest. It looks like the woods but on a psychedelic trip. The pinks, purples, and blues of various flowers wave and melt into the background, and I go walking for what feels like an exceptionally long time.

Finally, I break free from the woods and find myself in the center of a beautiful clearing. I stroll to the middle of it, and everything about it feels warm and familiar.

Then, from the tree line emerges a man.

He's beautiful. He's wearing blue jeans, but his upper half is unclothed. His muscular arms and chest move gracefully in the light as he makes his way over to me. He stands dangerously close to me, familiar gray eyes casting a mesmerizing spell on me as he draws nearer.

"Bailey …" he says, his voice trailing off. "Here I am."

"You … You're here," I say, the response flowing from this dreamy version of me. "Why are we here?"

"Where would you rather be?" he asks. His eyes are soft, attentive even.

"Home. I want to go home," I say firmly, and he takes my hand in his, his skin hot and radiant against my own.

In a subtle flash, the world spins, and we suddenly stand on the deck attached to my place. He opens the sliding glass door and pulls me inside, our fingers still interlocked.

He smiles as he asks, "Is this better?"

I nod. "Yeah. But how did you—"

"We can do whatever we want here, Bailey, in this dream space."

"Okay," I say softly. "Hey, I didn't ask you your name. You know mine, but I don't know yours."

He laughs, pulling us closer together. He grabs my other hand, bringing both to his face and kissing softly. "My name is Knox. Knox Roffe."

The next thing I know, my alarm goes off, pulling me from the dream as I force heavy eyelids to open and welcome the light of day. I blink, trying to process what happened, but bits of the dream slip away like sand between fingers with each passing second.

All I remember is his name.

Knox.

SEVEN

KNOX

The pull to her is inexorable.

Night and day, all I think about is her. I try hanging out at her cabin when she works and waiting for her to return, but the pull to her is consuming. I can hardly eat or sleep whenever she's not around, and I can't stand not knowing if she's safe. The other night was far too close of a call, and the thought of anything happening to her paralyzes me. I didn't realize that finding my mate could drive me to the brink of madness, but it has.

And I can't even show myself to her—my true self.

The thought angers me, but the feeling quickly dissipates with the sound of her car turning onto the long gravel drive. I can hear her coming from a mile away. My heart rattles madly in my chest, my body waiting for the scent of her sweet perfume to hit me before she's even out of the car.

"Hey, Wolfie," she says, my body flooded with excitement at how she flashes me that brilliant smile. I don't hate her calling me Wolfie, but I wish she knew me as Knox. It's weird, usually dream-sharing can only be done between packmates, but it seems the ability extends to a shifter's true mate as well.

Bailey settles into her usual routine, leaving the door open for me to sit in the doorway and keep her company as she makes dinner. She chats with me about her day, telling me all the best and worst bits, which customers were nice, and how her boss was a prick. Then, when she's done eating and cleaning up, she pats my head and says goodnight as I curl up and sleep on the deck, and she retires to her bedroom.

I let sleep take me quickly, eager to meet my love in the only space she can see me. Tonight, the dreamscape starts slow and inconspicuous. The two of us are walking down a sidewalk headed nowhere in particular. It looks like the city ... but nowhere I've been before. Bailey's hands are tucked into her pockets as we walk, the pungent smell of rain hanging in the cloudy sky.

"How do I always end up dreaming about you now, Knox? Ever since I met you that night in the clearing, I dream about you more nights than not."

I still haven't brought myself to tell her she's my mate. Or that I'm a shifter currently trapped in my wolf form due to the magic I utilized to bring us together.

For now, she thinks all this is a figment of her subconscious.

"I guess this is your way of making sense of having a wolf as your new protector," I tell her, and she smiles. "I must be the personification of that."

She wraps her arms around herself and squeezes, shivering. "I wish we were somewhere nicer for this dream."

"Here," I say. I stop on the sidewalk, large drops of rain now falling. They coat her lashes and drip down her cheeks, highlighting an inquisitive smirk that makes me want to nibble on her bottom lip. I hold my palms out, and she places her hands on mine. "Close your eyes."

I concentrate as a rush of warm air surrounds us, no time passing before we're standing somewhere new.

"Open your eyes," I say. She does, eyes wide and breath held as she looks around.

"It's beautiful," she says softly. "But how did you—"

"It's just a dream, Bailey. A mirage. Anything is possible here when we're together."

"I like that. Hey, Knox, can I ask you a question?"

"Anything," I tell her.

"Do you live in the woods? Where did you come from?"

I shrug. "I do live in the woods. I have a cabin that is not so different from yours. I have a ... community ... that I belong to, but I keep pretty much to myself anyway, so. What about you? Do you ever get lonely living in the woods?"

She smiles and shakes her head. "No. I have friends, and my best friend is great. We've been besties since we were little. But I like my peace and solitude. I like the quiet. I like the birds chirping. I feel more at home here than in the city, I guess."

"I guess we have that in common," I say. The way she smiles gives me butterflies, and I can't resist her lips any longer.

The humid air is warm and thick, leaving the taste of salt on her lips as I lean in and kiss her. She sighs against my mouth, wrapping her arms around my waist and pulling the two of us closer together as the kiss deepens.

"Come," I tell her, taking her hand and pulling her to the sandy beach. We sit down together, admiring the sunset. The glowing orb is half-covered by the horizon, but it won't sink lower than this. Here, in this dreamy state, everything is perfect. Everything *stays* perfect.

But she's perfect regardless of where we are.

I lean over and cup her face, admiring how her eyes shine when she looks at me. She's got this fire that comes out every time she smiles. I'd happily suffocate if that fire took up all the oxygen in the room.

I pull her face to mine, letting my lips linger in front of hers before finally letting them touch. She breathes deeply, her lips parting and welcoming my tongue into her mouth. I love the way she tastes salty and sweet and heavenly. I don't know if other humans taste this good, but I can't imagine it. I can't imagine anyone tasting better.

My mouth claims hers as I fight to keep from devouring her. Our lips tangle around one another, twisting and licking furiously in the deepening kiss. My hand snakes up into her lengthy hair, her raven locks tangling around my fingers as she moans quietly into my mouth. I feel a stirring in my pants at the way she kisses me back, her mouth as hungry and her body surely as needy as mine.

I so desperately want to have her, but ... not here, not like this.

I want her in person, flesh to flesh, skin to skin.

She breaks off the kiss and pulls away, a glimmer of worry in her eyes. "What's wrong?" Bailey asks.

I smile, not wanting to upset her or ruin this perfect, dreamy state with my impatient desires. "Nothing," I say, and it's almost true—life since I've found her has been night and day. Everything feels so much better when she's around. I hate having to wait for her to see the real me. I want to show her everything I am. I want to lay with her in bed and trace my fingertips along her skin. I want to have every inch of her, and I have no idea how long before I can make that happen.

"Okay," she replies, though she doesn't look like she entirely believes me.

I kiss her nose, then press my forehead to hers.

"Nothing is wrong when I'm with you," I tell her.

And I mean it.

EIGHT

BAILEY

My thighs clench together, the pulsing sensation between them making me quiver. It's not until my brain registers the incessant ringing as my alarm that I open my eyes. My room is softly aglow with the morning light, and how my leg muscles gently ache indicates how much I was squeezing them throughout the night.

This time, more of the dream stays with me even as I grow more awake.

The man on the beach ... Knox ... we were watching the sunset and making out, and god, was it hot. It felt so real; I can almost still taste his mouth on mine. My body doesn't seem to realize it was only a dream either, as I feel the subtle dampness of arousal between my thighs and moan.

Gosh.

I never wanted that dream to end. Damn alarm. I wonder if Knox and I would have taken things any farther. It's been a couple of months since I've been with anyone since Zach and I broke up. I haven't been on a single date or so much as kissed anyone, never mind having gotten laid. Maybe that's why my brain is manifesting this dream man. Perhaps it's trying to tell me I need to focus more on self-care.

I pee and then head to the central part of my place, opening my front door to my new favorite view every morning.

"Hey, Wolfie," I say, and he whines at me happily. I leave the door open, and he sits in the doorway as I fix myself some eggs and toast.

"Guys are the worst, you know? I mean, human guys. Like my ex, Zach. You know what he did? He cheated on me. And not, like, once. Several times. Every single time he went out of town for a work trip during the last year of our relationship, if not before that. At least, that's what one of the girls he slept with told me. I guess he told her he was single, and then she saw a picture of us together online. Can you believe that?"

He cocks his head, his gray eyes seeming a bit sad compared to usual. I dip my toast into one of my eggs, coating it in yolk before popping it in my mouth. "And you know ... you know what else?" I say between chewing, "he tried to blame it on me! Can you ... Can you believe that? How rude is that? As if *I* was the problem when he's the one who never wanted sex. It's not like I didn't try to proposition him. I like sex. It's just ... Maybe it's because I put on a few pounds in our last year together? I don't know."

He whines loudly, both his front paws clawing at the air. "You think I look good, right? I think so, too. Ugh, I'm sorry, Wolfie. I don't even know why I'm telling you all this." I scarf down the rest of my food. "I need to shower and get ready for work."

———

When I get home that night, Wolfie is sitting on my deck exactly where he was when I left. I crouch down beside him and rub his head a few times before I open my door. I go inside and throw my purse and keys down, grab myself a beer from the fridge, and sit out in a chair on the deck for a bit.

Wolfie comes and lays at my bare feet, the warmth of his body radiating into my toes and making me smile.

"It's nice out here," I say, his ears perking slightly. "I love it out here. I was fortunate when I rented this place. There were several other applicants, you know. I rented it with my ex, but he ... Well, he didn't care to live out here. I believe '*bullshit middle of nowhere*' were the words he used. God, I should have left him then. Anyone who hates nature that much is a walking red flag in my books.

"But I guess I thought it was alright since he was away for work so much. He didn't live with me out here full-time. And now ... Now no one lives with me out here. Minus you, I guess, since you seem to be staying around."

He cranes his head up at me, those big gray eyes as warm and soothing as the rest of him. He lays his head in my lap, my fingers instinctively scratching the spot behind his ears he's so fond of.

"You like living out here with me, don't you, boy?"

Wolfie whines and nuzzles his nose against the crook of my elbow.

I scoff. "You're probably a thousand times more loyal than what my shitty ex ever was. I'm glad I'm single. I'm glad it's just you and me out here, and I don't have to worry about having a man around who will break my heart anyway."

Wolfie headbutts my knee, then raises a giant paw and scrapes it across my lap. "See? You love me, don't you? That's why you come here and cuddle me at the end of the day. And that's why you're always here in the morning. It's nice." I sigh. "Animals are better than people, Wolfie."

Wolfie howls loudly, sending birds in nearby trees scattering across the dimming sky. I check my watch and realize it's getting late. "Well, I better get inside and get ready for bed." As if by command, Wolfie backs off and gives me room to get up. He watches me as I head back inside, turning to him as I hold the door half-open.

"Goodnight, Wolfie," I say, and he howls in response, locking those smoky gray eyes on mine until the door is shut.

NINE

KNOX

I stare in her window as she pulls the duvet further up and tucks it under her chin. She looks so peaceful when she sleeps, but the best part is that I can join her and meet up with her in the dreamscape once she's good and out.

It's still wild to me that it's even possible. I've heard of sets of shifters meeting there, but I had no idea it was possible between a shifter-human couple. Bailey's a natural at navigating it, too. I've been helping her change our placement or what we're doing, and she's gotten the hang of it.

I curl up on the deck, letting myself drift off into a deep sleep until the world twists and turns and the dreamscape slowly starts forming in front of my eyes.

I watch as the empty white space of my mind is quickly replaced by flowing red drapes, a patterned armchair, a plush-looking king-size bed, and an old-school clawfoot tub surrounded by tile in an otherwise carpeted room. Other details form, and I'm left spinning around in awe, genuinely impressed that Bailey built all this just with her imagination.

"Hello, handsome," a voice comes from behind me—her voice.

The room has transformed into a luxury hotel room. A

bucket full of ice with an expensive bottle of champagne is atop the dresser. Rose petals suddenly litter the floor, and Bailey stands there wearing a slinky black dress with a grin on her face. "May I?" I ask, reaching towards her. She enthusiastically nods.

I let my fingers trace down the silky sheen of the satin fabric. I use a light touch to caress the bare skin of a shoulder, down her arm, and across her stomach. Every bit of her feels fantastic, and I don't protest when she presses her body up against mine and kisses me hard.

I let my hands get lost in her hair as we make out, the two of us kissing like high schoolers in a frenzy. I can hardly help myself when my hands fall to the hem of her dress and lift it slowly, teasing the bare skin of her legs with the slightest touch. A soft moan from her reverberates through our kiss, the front of my pants tightening as I grow hard with need.

"Bailey," I say against her mouth, but she presses a finger to my lips.

"Please, Knox," she whispers, "don't overthink it."

I watch her as she turns and heads for the bed. She crawls into it on all fours, a sight that has me throbbing. She turns to face me, letting her arms fall out to the sides as she smiles at me with a devilish look.

"Come lay with me," she asks, and I'm happy to oblige.

I get in bed beside her, propping my head on one elbow as I admire her form. My other hand wanders again, sliding over her knee and thigh as I gently hike her dress up around her hips. The black dress scoots up enough to reveal a pair of bright red panties, my cock twitching hard at the sight.

She looks delicious, and I can't resist the ravenous hunger she fuels in me any longer.

I sit up beside her. I watch her eyes grow smoky with lust as I hook my thumbs under the sides of her panties and begin to roll them down her voluptuous thighs. My mouth waters at the thought of tasting her sweet juices., but I take my time undressing her. I slip her panties off her feet and inhale her scent a moment before tossing them to the floor. Then I sit her up and pull her dress off over her head, her naked body draped across the bed as she lays back down.

"Knox," she says breathily, "will you make love to me?"

I shake my head. "No," I answer softly. "Tonight will be just about you. About me spoiling you."

I think I see a hint of disappointment in her eyes, but it quickly vanishes as I trail kisses around her knees and up her inner thighs. Her skin is hot on my lips, her thighs quivering slightly whenever my lips press against them. I watch as she wiggles and squirms, her hips raising from the bed slightly the closer I get to her core.

Finally, I kiss over her mound and down her slit, her body nearly jumping off the bed with the way she presses her hips forward. She's already begun to glisten in anticipation, and the sound that escapes her is pure hunger when my tongue finally slides up the length of her opening. Her juices coat my tongue and make me want her more. I let my fingers sink into her hips, guiding her pussy harder into my mouth as my tongue parts her and presses its way inside.

"Oh god," she cries out when my tongue slides up over her clit. I draw slow circles around it, and she moans loudly. I tease her like this for a while. I like the way she grows wetter as my tongue laps around her sweet spot, but I also really want to make her experience a level of ecstasy she's never had before.

Her breath halts as I tease her opening with one of my fingers. I keep my mouth planted on her, sucking and nibbling on her swollen clit as her hips drive up toward my finger. I can tell how badly she needs this, how her body yearns for touch with its responsiveness. I press a thick finger inside her, and she moans, letting her adjust to the feeling as her tight walls clasp around and push my finger further inside.

Her moaning turns to ragged pants as I slide the finger in and out, in and out. She's wet as hell now, her juices coating my lips and tongue as I begin licking her furiously. I slowly press a second finger inside, and she moans, her hips starting to tremble as the fullness, coupled with the clitoral stimulation, begins to drive her closer and closer to orgasm.

Her hips move up to meet the thrusts of my fingers. I use my other hand to cup her ass and keep her pressed against my lips, savoring the way her wetness begins covering my face. Her panting turns to sharp cries of pleasure, her fingernails digging into the bed's duvet as she screams my name.

"Fuck, Knox, I'm coming! Oh, Knox, yes!"

I hungrily drink up her pleasure as her thighs tighten and her hips buck with release. She coats me in her juices, and I love it.

I love it more when I set her back down on the bed, and she stares up at me with that insatiable hunger, pulling me up to meet her face and kissing me hard as she licks the taste of herself from my lips.

I kiss her temple, smiling at the way she lays there, a contented mess with half-closed eyes.

I can't wait to be able to shift again. I *need* to be able to shift again.

I can't wait to do all this and more with her in person.

TEN

BAILEY

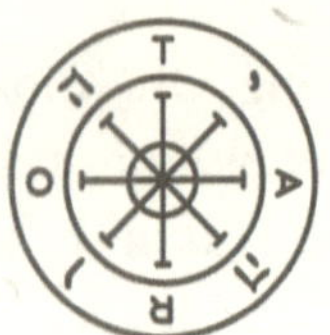

The last hour of my shifts ticks by as I reminisce about the dream I had last night. Knox going down on me was the hottest thing I've experienced since … I don't even know when.

Zach was a prude and a dickhead, and our sex life was never particularly robust. He never wanted to experiment or try new things. He never wanted to do anything even remotely kinky. He just wanted plain old vanilla sex. I guess it's really for the best we didn't work out.

But … I think I need to get laid.

That dream left me so flustered. I woke up with soaked panties and a shortness of breath. It was like I had the damn orgasm. Who knows—Maybe I did.

My shift ends, but I don't leave the store. Instead, I shop, picking up coffee, milk, eggs, and all of my usual things, plus a few things on sale. Then I turn down an aisle I never go down, the sheer volume of it feeling a tad overwhelming.

I scour the shelves. The bags come in all different colors and sizes, all bearing labels with ingredients and their supposed benefits. I stand there debating which to pick, finally settling for one that claims to have only whole ingredients and primarily beef.

I don't know if a wolf will eat dog food, but I'm worried Wolfie hasn't been eating or eating enough.

I buy the food and head home for the day. The bag of dog food sits in the passenger seat, a stark reminder of how much I may be losing it. "God, I think I've lost my mind," I huff, glancing at the food, then back at the road. "Fuck. What is going on with me lately?"

I pull into my place, and there's Wolfie. He's sitting on the deck waiting for me, as he has been every night and morning since our first encounter. I grab the food and hop out, bending down to scratch behind his ear once I'm near.

"How was your day, boy? You were out here all day again, weren't you?"

I love how he presses his head harder against my hand, his soft fur brushing between my fingers. He sits in the doorway as I head inside, watching me as I kick off my shoes and head to the kitchen. I find a bowl and fill it with food, bringing it out on the deck and setting it in front of him. "There you go. Do you want that? The bag says beef is the main ingredient, Wolfie. Might not be as good as the real thing, but it's better than going hungry, right?"

He stares into the bowl for a moment before shoving his nose into the edge of it and pushing it back towards me. He paws at the kibbles, spilling some onto the deck as he whines loudly.

"You don't want it?" I sigh. "Just what am I going to do with you, Wolfie? You can't not eat because you spend all your time outside my place. Silly wolf." His shoulders straighten and then slump again as if in some makeshift shrug.

But wolves don't shrug ... Do they?

I sit down in a deck chair and sigh. I'm out of ideas short of going into the woods and trying to hunt critters myself. But I'm no huntress, and the thought of killing anything brings a tear to my eye.

An idea hits me, and I smile. "You know what? Plan B, Wolfie." I spring from my chair and dash inside the kitchen. I whip up a healthy dinner, skipping salt or any seasoning. I throw a bunch of steak strips, rice, and veggies onto two plates. Then I set one outside and wait, but Wolfie glances at it before continuing to stare at me.

"Alright, suit yourself then. I'm starving, so I'm eating."

I no sooner finish my dinner than Wolfie's nose is in his plate, scarfing down every last crumb and licking the dish clean.

"Did you seriously wait for me to finish before eating?" I ask with a laugh. "You're a strange wolf." I sigh deeply. "No stranger than me, I guess. I keep having these dreams about ... a man. A gorgeous man."

Wolfie's ears perk up. His head cocks to the side as he looks at me. I feel silly telling a wolf all my problems and weird dreams, but it's not like I have anyone else to talk to. Cassie is busy getting ready for her wedding. I can't bombard her with my problems. And all our other friends are in long-term relationships and wouldn't get it.

"I can't stop thinking about him, Wolfie. I don't know why. I just ... feel so drawn to him. You probably think that's ridiculous, being attached to some dream man. He's not even real."

Wolfie whines and paws the air. I don't know what it is, but sometimes I swear he understands me and gets what I'm going through. It's like he's become my best friend in a certain sense, always there when I get home, always there to lend an ear while I vent about all the weird bullshit in my life.

I go collect his plate. I put all the dishes in the sink, leaving them for tomorrow. The day has felt long, and thinking back on the dream and my relationship with Zach has left me feeling worn out. I've sworn off men and dating, and for good reason. I need to focus on myself and work on healing from my shitty relationship with Zach.

And yet, I'm silently praying I dream about Knox again tonight.

ELEVEN

I'm surprised by Bailey's choice of venue this time in the dreamscape.

I look around, every detail of the space meticulously accurate and already so familiar. The walls of her open-concept house greet us. The bookshelf stacked with romances, murder mysteries, and a few cookbooks sits in the corner, every title accounted for. The open spaces on each wall are decorated with abstract paintings, collages, and photos of her and her friends.

The kitchen island has a fruit dish, complete with apples and oranges. The TV sits on its stand, and her velvety couch, with its many blankets and pillows, is in front of it. Everything is here, perfectly curated from her memory.

We sit together on the couch and sip hot cocoa that she's made, the silence of the late-night hour creeping in from outside and filling the house. A corner lamp brings warmth to the room while the near-full moon cascades blocks of light along the floor of the eastern wall. I sip the cocoa, enjoying its heat and the way it's rich but not too sweet.

"I'm happy I'm dreaming about you again, Knox," she says past the edge of her mug as she blows on the hot liquid.

"Yeah?" I try not to sound too eager and fail miserably. "And why is that? Not that I'm complaining."

"I don't really have anyone else to talk to about everything," she explains. "I have Cassie, of course, but she's been so busy planning her wedding. And she's happy; she's in a good place right now. I don't want to bring her down by constantly discussing my problems. And our other friends ... I don't think they'd get it. They'd just tell me to move on. With the best of intentions, but they'd make it sound so damn easy, and ... it's not. Not after what Zach put me through."

I scoot a little closer to her on the couch, happy when I wrap an arm over her shoulders, and she leans her head into my chest. "It sounds like he put you through a lot mentally and emotionally."

"He did," she says thoughtfully, eyes cast off in some distant memory. "He really did. He was awful to me. I don't know why I stayed with him as long as I did. Just scared of being alone, I guess."

"That's fair. And there's no shame in that," I assure her.

She looks up at me, confused. "You don't think so?"

"No. What's wrong with not wanting to be alone?"

She rests her head back down against me. "I don't know. I guess I've always thought I should be a *strong, independent woman*, you know? Like I'm supposed to be able to take on the world's weight by myself and grin and bear it. But it gets hard, feeling so alone all the time. Which is funny since I choose to live in a cabin in the woods rather than in the city, but ... There's a difference between being *alone* and being *lonely*, I think."

"I know what you mean," I say.

And I do.

I've been around for a long, long time, as many shifters have, and I've been looking for my fated mate since day one. Even when my packmates surround me, the underlying sting of loneliness is always there. That's why I'm happy I finally have Bailey in my life.

It took me so much longer than I anticipated to find her. Bailey has no idea how long I waited.

That's why, as much as I hate it, sacrificing my ability to shift for a bit was worth it. Using Agatha and her tarot deck was worth it.

The Wheel was worth it.

I debate telling Bailey about the tarot cards and how I found her but think better of it. "I think everyone wants to find love," I say. "Or, at least, most people. And I don't think there's anything wrong with that. Wanting to be loved. Wanting to have someone you can depend on. All of that is important."

She smiles up at me. "I think you're right." She sighs, "I guess I've just always had shit luck when it comes to picking men."

"Maybe that's finally come to an end," I say softly.

She cocks a brow. "Oh? No offense, Knox, but I don't think manifesting my dream man every night in my dreams counts as finding myself a man in the real world. Pretty sure my friends would throw me in an insane asylum if I told them, which is another reason I'm keeping it to myself."

I shift away from her, taking her mug and mine and setting them both on the coffee table. "I need to show you something."

A confused look sets over her pretty features, but she says nothing else. I grab her by the hand and take her through the house, out the glass patio doors, until she's standing on the deck.

"Knox, what are you ... Why are we—"

I step off the deck and turn around. I concentrate, feeling the familiar buzz of magic coursing through me as my body shifts and morphs into its animalistic form. A flash of light floods the night. Bailey shields her eyes as the light gives way to darkness, her eyes adjusting as all that's left is the moonlight and me, coming up to her shoulders as I stand on all fours in front of her.

Her eyes are vast, but there isn't any fear in them. Instead, they're filled with curiosity. Surprise. A million questions, questions that sit on her open mouth but that her lips fail to form into tangible words.

"Knox, I ... But you ..."

"I've wanted to show you this since we met, Bailey Dennis. I'm a—"

But I don't get the word *shifter* out before the familiar blaring of her alarm pierces the air, and we're both ripped away from the dreamscape.

TWELVE

Ho-ly crap.

My mind is still reeling from that crazy dream. I reach over and shut off the still-blaring alarm on my phone. My heart beats a million miles a minute, a residual hot sweat licking my brow. I fight my way out of tangled sheets and head to the bathroom. I flick the light on and splash some cold water on my face, expecting to look tired as hell, but all that greets me are unexpectedly bright eyes and cheeks flushed with the rosy afterglow of what just happened.

What *I dreamt* happened.

I splash more water. I need to get a grip. Wolfie isn't Knox disguised as a wolf. I didn't just have the most fantastic oral of my life with my dream man. None of it happened; none of it is true. It's all just my imagination screaming at me to go out and get laid.

With a *real* man, not a dream one.

I look at myself again and smile. I'm happy I don't look hideous today. It's Cassie's wedding day, and there's sure to be some single hotties somewhere in her or her husband's families. And, as the maid of honor, it shouldn't be hard for those hotties to find me.

I take a shower and do my hair and makeup. Then I put on

the blush-colored gown Cassie and I picked out and check myself out in the full-length mirror in my bedroom.

I look *HOT*.

I gather my purse and keys and get ready to head out. Wolfie is in his usual spot on the deck but immediately sits up from where he's lying when I open the door. "What do you think, boy?" I ask, and he whines, pawing excitedly at the air before him. "You approve? Good."

I spin slowly for him, letting him see the dress from every angle. The way he watches me, head cocked and eyes fixated, somehow reminds me of the dream I had last night. It's weird, when I look into his eyes ... I could swear they look exactly like the gray eyes of the man in my dreams.

But that's the thing with dreams, isn't it? They pull from your conscious mind, taking bits here and there from your day-to-day life and mashing them together in some nonsensical sequence for your brain to play you later. I must have manufactured the man's eyes based on Wolfie's. That's a fair explanation for the uncanny resemblance.

I do one last spin. "Verdict? Do I look good enough to eat?" Wolfie chuffs loudly. "Good. I need to look like absolute fire tonight. I think there's going to be at least a couple of hot guys there, and I need to get laid. Like, desperately."

Wolfie's ears pin back as he lowers his body to the deck and growls. I freeze, standing across from him on the deck. He keeps growling, his eyes bright with a spark of madness that turns my blood cold and forms a lump in my throat. I've never seen him like this or anything but docile. I've heard of seemingly domesticated wild animals turning feral on humans without notice.

But Wolfie wouldn't do that. I know he'd never do anything to harm me.

I don't know how I know. I just *know*.

"Settle down, boy," I tell him, my feet suddenly a thousand pounds each. "I don't bring hookups back here, so you have nothing to worry about."

Wolfie keeps growling as I watch him. I walk over to him cautiously and crouch down, stroking his fur as I stare into his eyes. Then I smile, a gesture which seems to settle his nerves and calm him down finally. He looks at me, but there's no anger in his eyes. There's nothing but endless gray pools of ... concern.

"Hey, boy. Seriously, you don't have to worry. I'm never going to bring anyone else back here. Besides, I don't even know if there will be cute guys. I assume there are. Anyway, you shouldn't get riled up about it."

He licks my face, and I laugh. It strikes me as odd that he would even understand what I mean. How would a wolf possibly know what a hookup is? How would he know what it means when I talk about whether or not I ever bring others here? And why is he so opposed? Just out of concern for my safety?

I look into his eyes one more time, their intensity pulling my mind back to the dreamland where I experienced more pleasure than anyone's ever brought me. But a wolf shouldn't remind me of such things, and I shake the thought from my mind. I can't let the lines of reality be blurred with these weird dreams I've been having, regardless of how realistic they may feel.

I see my rideshare pulling up and lock my door. "I'll see you later, Wolfie," I tell him, giving him a few more head rubs before I get in the back of the car. I turn and watch him as we pull away. He doesn't move from the deck. He sits there, his eyes glued to the car until he's entirely out of sight. I'm not sure that poor creature has left the deck once since he found me. And, no matter how much I might think it's weird or try to deny it, I've been happy to have him around.

I never pegged myself for a dog person, but he's comforting and pleasant to talk to and makes me feel safe. And his presence somehow feels more human than animal to me. He might not be the beautiful man from my dreams, but I don't want him to leave. I mean, he *can't* be the beautiful man from my dreams. It's impossible.

Isn't it?

THIRTEEN

KNOX

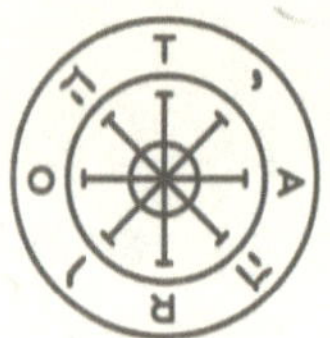

My mind is screaming at me to run.

I watch the car drive away; Bailey turns in the backseat and looks at me until the car turns past some trees, and I can't see her anymore.

No way in hell am I letting some random guy at this wedding hook up with *my* mate.

I debate following the car. I can still hear it in the distance, so it wouldn't be too late to catch up and keep enough distance so that Bailey doesn't notice me. But my body is vibrating with frustration. I can't stand the thought of her with someone else, but how do I intervene if it comes to that? Just show up and potentially crash her best friend's wedding? No doubt that'd make her hate me.

I let out a loud howl, desperate to release some pent-up frustration, when a familiar feeling gnaws at the pit of my stomach with ferocity. I feel my power come flooding back, my body twitching and shifting as clumps of fur fall away. It seems the magic leeched from me every day I couldn't shift has finally paid the tarot's toll. Paws turn to hands, and I find myself back in human form, stark naked on Bailey's deck, with the sunlight caressing every bit of my bare skin.

Fuck, I've missed this.

I love how it feels to stand and move on two feet again. I stretch my arms over my head and wiggle the stiffness out of my limbs as I shift my weight from side to side. It feels so damn good to be me again.

And more importantly, the me that Bailey needs and deserves.

I look around, unsure of what I should do for clothes. I don't have any here, and my house is too far away to stop there. I'll miss too much of the wedding and risk Bailey meeting someone or something ... happening.

I force the thought out of my head as I look at her kitchen window. From what I've seen, she never locks it. She probably feels she doesn't need to, living way out here. I press my hands to the glass and slide, happy when it opens easily. I climb through and over the counter, my feet thudding softly on the wooden floor.

I wander through the house, this delightful feeling of contentment overtaking me. I've sat in the cabin's doorway many times, watching her while she goes about her day, but I've never stepped inside. The place is flooded with scents and signs of her. Little notes on the fridge in her handwriting. Things she leaves lying about, like hair ties and books. I like gathering this story of her life, imagining her in the rooms I'd not seen, like the bathroom and bedroom.

Her bedroom is painted a smoky blue, not at all what I expected. Little pops of pastel yellow in pillows, a throw blanket, and the drapes give a touch of warmth to the space. The way the space is decorated is simple but beautiful, and my brain can't help but wander to thoughts of the two of us falling to sleep together in her bed each night, my arm draped over her waist and her tucked against me.

I open the armoire across from the bed and find what I'm looking for—A few complete sets of men's clothes. I grab a pair of blue jeans that look like they'll fit and a plain T-shirt. It must be the remnants of her ex, some scraps of clothing he didn't care for enough to pick up. It works out well for me that we're about the same size, though the shirt is more snug around the biceps than I'd prefer. They have some residual douchebag stink to them as well, but beggars can't be choosers.

I snoop around the house until I find the wedding invitation. I note the address and take off on foot, needing to arrive in the city dressed to pick up some better clothes. It's a good thing I stashed my phone and wallet in the woods nearby when I realized I'd be staying at Bailey's for a while. I need to pick out a proper suit if I'm going to impress Bailey at this wedding. Traveling in wolf form would be faster, but I'll tear all these clothes if I shift in them. Still, even on two feet, I'm far faster than any human could ever be.

I dig up my wallet and race to the city. I know a good central spot for suits that isn't too far from the venue. I head there and buy something off the rack, and it fits me surprisingly well for not being custom-tailored. I look in the mirror and smile, admiring how the dark gray fabric compliments my light gray eyes. I look damn sharp, and I can't help but smile at the thought of what her reaction is going to be.

If seeing me like this doesn't impress Bailey, nothing will.

I toss her ex's clothes in a garbage can and head for the venue. It's several blocks away, but walking there doesn't take me too long. The wedding is at a local church, the outside of the place decorated in blush-colored roses, but all the fun will be at Cassie's hotel reception. Every detail is immaculate, and I already know how stunning the gorgeous woman waiting for me inside is.

My heart is beating so fast I feel dizzy. It's not like me to get nervous around women, but something about Bailey is different. Something about her makes me so badly want to impress her, woo her, and sweep her off her feet in a way she's never experienced before.

It's like what I did in that dream the other night.

The large, arched wooden doors of the church are tightly closed, but I swing them open and head inside. I enter the main lobby and coat check area, crossing it without a glance. Then I realize I hear music coming from the upper level, so I follow the noise upstairs and investigate. Everyone is spread out in a wide-open room that I'm sure hardly gets utilized for anything other than weddings and community board meetings.

I wander around, offering polite nods and smiles to the other patrons.

And then I see her. Bailey Dennis, my fated mate. And she's all the more stunning up close.

I'm not sure I was ready for this.

Fourteen

Bailey

"Seriously, you look beautiful," I gush, swiping a tear from my eye.

"Don't go getting all mushy on me now!" Cassie throws her arms around my neck, and we dance together playfully.

"Shouldn't you be dancing with your new husband?"

Cassie looks over, my eyes following hers. "Nah, he looks pretty cozy sitting there teaching his mom how to use her new iPhone. I think he's good. Besides, he got the first dance. He can't have *all* the dances." We both giggle. "The real question is, will *you* dance with anyone else?"

My stomach somersaults when I see Zach, my ex, quickly approaching. "I know who I'm not dancing with, that's for sure. I can't believe he showed up here."

Cassie's face scrunches in an apologetic look. "I'm so sorry, Bay. Obviously, we invited him when you guys were still a thing and ... well, he was kinda a friend before that, but I'd have preferred he not come."

"I know," I tell her, squeezing her hand. "Seriously, it's fine."

Zach walks up to us, the greasiest smirk plastered on his face.

"Ladies," he says, but his eyes are focused solely on me. "You look like you could use a dancing partner, Bee."

"I'm going to go get a drink," Cassie mutters with sympathetic eyes. "You okay?"

"Oh yeah, I'm good. Can you grab me one, too?" I ask her. "Just whatever you're having."

She nods and hurries off to the bar.

"So, Bee," Zach continues, "how have you been?"

"*Stop* calling me that," I hiss through gritted teeth, "and I've been fine, not that you care."

"Ouch," he says. "Of course, I care. I think—"

"I think you should leave now," I interject. "You shouldn't have come here. This is *my* best friend's wedding."

"I just wanted to apologize and ask you to dance," he pouts.

"I don't need your apologies, Zach, and no way in hell am I dancing with you."

His brows furrow, and his thin lips curl into a tight frown. That look, the same look he would give whenever I called him out for lying or cheating or gaslighting, immediately pisses me off, but I keep my cool. "You just gonna dance with Cassie all night, then?"

"Would that be such a bad thing?" I snap. "I don't *need* a man to dance with, Zach. Unlike you, I can have fun solo and don't get my validation from the opposite sex."

"How dare you!" he hisses, anger flashing through his dark eyes. "You're not perfect, Bee. Stop talking to me like you're some holy saint, and I'm the scum of the earth. All I wanted was one dance."

I fold my arms over my chest. "I already said I don't want to dance with you, Zach."

His face softens. "Please, Bee? For old time's sake?" His hands pull at my arms to unfold them.

I snap my arms back, tucking my hands into my armpits. "Don't touch me!"

Cassie comes back, holding two drinks. "Hey, I got you a tequila sunrise. That okay?"

"Amazing," I say, taking the drink with a smile. I shoot Zach a death glare. "Too busy enjoying this lovely beverage to dance with you. Sorry, Zach."

"Who is *that*?" Cassie gasps, pointing.

I turn and see a man headed straight for us. His dark gray suit is sharp and well-cut around broad shoulders and a thick chest. He runs his fingers through brown hair that is sexily messy. When he gets closer, I can see that his eyes are the most unique shade I've ever seen, a light gray that catches the light and brings a depth both intimidating and intoxicating.

He looks so familiar, and yet I can't place him.

He walks up to the three of us, ignoring Zach and Cassie as his eyes meet mine. "Hi," he says, his deep voice rumbling the pit of my stomach and catching my breath.

"Hi," I say back. I clear my throat. "Do I know you?"

"Would you like to dance?" he asks. He ignores my question, but the way he's smiling at me, I don't care.

"Just who the heck are you?" Zach demands, trying to position himself between me and the mystery man. "She's already planning to dance with—"

"Can you hold my drink?" I ask Cassie, and her eyes grow wide.

She looks between the gorgeous stranger and me and nods. "Yeah! Of course. Sure. Yeah. Go! Have fun! I'll be at the bar." She takes my drink and scurries, leaving me with the two men.

"I said she's not interested," Zach says, but the man folds his arms over his chest. He's several inches taller, towers over Zach, and clearly has a lot of weight on him. Zach shrinks back. "Right, Bee?" he asks, still looking at the stranger.

"Come on," the man says, sidestepping Zach and holding out a hand.

I place my hands in his, immediately taken by how their warmth wraps around me and travels up the length of my arms.

The look on Zach's face is priceless as I let the stranger whisk me away to the center of the dance floor, but I hardly notice. I'm too busy taking in every detail of this man's face, trying to place where I've seen those chiseled, rugged features before.

And those eyes. Those damn eyes.

They pull me in as he looks down at me. My whole body tingles at the feel of his large hand as it presses into my lower back, his other hand gently caressing one of mine. I place my free hand on his shoulder, smiling as his feet move around the floor, and I gracefully follow suit.

The rest of the room melts away with the way he watches me. There are so many things I want to ask where he's from. What his favorite restaurant is. Who invited him to Cassie's wedding? A million thoughts race through my mind, but my mouth settles on the most straightforward words.

"Who are you?"

He smiles. "Knox. Knox Roffe."

FIFTEEN

I see her, and my heart jumps.

She lights up the room in that blush-colored gown, her full figure hugged in all the right places. She looked magnificent when she was spinning for me on the deck in wolf form, but somehow, she seems all the more divine now that I'm a man.

I make my way across the room. A woman and a man stand around her. I gather the woman must be Cassie, the bride. She's in a feathered wedding gown that would make any man proud to have her hanging off their arm, yet she still pales compared to Bailey.

A closer look reveals Bailey's frustrated expression. Her mouth sits in a hard line, arms folded across her chest as the man next to her patters on. He tries to pull her arms away, but she snatches them back, my blood boiling at his audacity.

How dare he touch my mate, especially when the touch is so unwelcome.

Thoughts of physically dragging the man out and beating the shit out of him in the parking lot flash through my mind. But Bailey is here to celebrate and support her friend Cassie, and the last thing that'll strengthen the bond between us is me making a scene. I take a few deep, calming breaths before forcing a broad smile and approaching them.

"Hi," I say, ignoring Cassie and the man. I can't help but give her a hundred percent of my attention, and she seems to return the favor when eager eyes meet mine and she smiles.

"Hi," she says back, clearing her throat. "Do I know you?"

It shouldn't, but it tickles me that her brain must be scrambling to figure out who I am and how she recognizes me. I want to tell her everything but now isn't the time or place. Jogging her memory back to the times we've shared through the dreamscape will have to happen organically over time. I don't want to overwhelm or scare her away. After all, she's human and likely has no idea that shifters exist.

"Would you like to dance?" I ask, opting to change the subject. I need to get her away from this dickhead who keeps glaring at me. And I really, really need to get her pressed up against me in that dress.

"Just who the heck are you?" the man asks snarkily. He tries to wedge himself between Bailey and me, but there's no chance he'd overpower me in a physical altercation. Not even if I was also human. "She's already planning to dance with—"

"Can you hold my drink?" Bailey asks Cassie, and I can't help but grin at how she blatantly ignores his intervention.

"Yeah! Of course. Sure. Yeah. Go! Have fun. I'll be at the bar," Cassie replies, taking Bailey's drink and hurrying off, leaving the three of us in an awkward triangle.

"I said she's not interested," he pipes up. He folds his arms over his chest, but it's more pathetic than intimidating. He's several inches shorter than I am and not nearly as wide. "Right, Bee?" he asks, eyes fixed on me. I don't even bother looking at him.

The only thing in this room worth looking at is her; I want to ensure she knows it.

"Come on," I say, sidestepping the shrimp of a human and

holding my hand out. I feel my heart thump in my chest as she places her delicate hand in mine, hands I've felt scratch behind my ears and run along my fur.

Hands I've *felt* before, but never skin-to-skin.

Her fingertips feel electric against my own, her cool skin melting against my own heat. I wrap my hand around hers protectively and whisk her off to the dance floor, eager to get away from everyone else. I'm keen to know what it feels like to have her close, to dance with her now that I'm back on human legs.

I grab the small of her back and hold her other hand. She puts her free hand on my shoulder, the two of us naturally falling into place together as I move my feet and lead her around the floor. A few other couples are dancing, but the floor is spacious, and I'm happy to utilize it to take broad steps as the two of us become passionate storms flurrying around the room.

"Who are you?" she asks. Her smile is brilliant, and her eyes are aglow with curiosity as they trace the various features of my face.

I can't lie to her nor resist the truth any longer.

"Knox. Knox Roffe."

Her brows pinch together slightly, pouty lips puckering in thought. "Wait ... Why does that sound so familiar? Have we met before? Have I helped you at the grocery store downtown?"

I can't help but laugh. "No, I'm not a patron of the grocery store."

"Then how ... how do I know you?"

I can't lie, but I'm not ready to answer all her questions either. Instead, I opt to plant the softest kiss on her lips, pulling away to gauge her reaction.

Her cheeks are rosy, but an undeniable hunger in her eyes makes my body stiffen.

I kiss her again, and she kisses me back, her mouth eagerly taking in my bottom lip and sucking on it gently. Soon, the only bits of us dancing are our tongues, our mouths hungrily exploring the other's in ways we've only dreamed about. Literally.

But the way she tastes puts every encounter in the dreamscape to shame. Her sweetness fills my mouth and brings with it subtle hints of tequila. Of all the humans I could have been fated to, I can't imagine one half as perfect as her.

And now, with the debt to the tarot paid and my shifting ability reinstated, I can finally have her.

SIXTEEN

BAILEY

I don't protest when he leans in, hot breath tickling my ear, and whispers, "Come with me."

The hotel is bustling with wedding attendees and other patrons, but I don't feel nervous as Knox pulls me through the crowds. He navigates his way down a hall, me in tow, with our hands clasped tightly together. I wish I knew his thoughts, but I'm also somewhat curious. I follow along quietly, my brows raising when we approach an unmarked door at the end of a long hall on the main floor.

"What is this? It's not a hotel room," I say, tickled by how amused he looks.

"Do you trust me?" he asks.

"Yes," I say, and I do. I don't know why; I can't explain it. But somehow, deep down, I know I can trust him.

"Come on," he says. He looks around to ensure no one's watching us, then opens the door and pulls me inside. He shuts the door behind us, the room turning to complete darkness for a second as he fumbles around to find the light switch.

When he flicks it, I see we're standing in an oversized storage closet. There are shelves stacked high with hotel amenities: toilet paper, boxes of miniature shampoo and soap bottles, and other bits and bobs a hotel would need. I feel a sudden surge of energy, excitement, and nervousness.

"Now, just why did you bring me in here?" I ask, shooting him a playful smile.

He gives me a mischievous look, but there's a hunger in his eyes that creates a dampness between my thighs. "I just needed to get you alone for a second," he says. He comes over and cups my face, tilting my head to the side and letting his lips graze along my outstretched neck. I shudder. "There were too many people on that dance floor for me to ravish you properly."

"Is that what you're wanting?" I ask breathily. "To ravish me?"

"Only if that's okay with you, Miss Dennis."

He trails kisses along my neck and behind my ear, my whole body aching with overwhelming desire. I let my hands land on his firm chest, the fabric of his suit jacket smooth against my fingertips. Despite the layers of his shirt and jacket, I can feel his muscular form, and I yearn to know what his arms and torso look like unclothed. But getting naked in the closet would be far too risky, and I've just met this man.

Haven't I?

He nibbles my earlobe, causing me to moan loudly. I can feel how wet my panties are growing with every touch, and everything about him leaves me wanting more. My lips are parted when his mouth finds mine, and I am desperate to taste him again.

He kisses me hard and deep. Both his hands trail down the front of my dress, over my breasts, as his fingertips graze my nipples. I opted to go braless, and the satin lining of my dress rubbing against my hardening nipples only further drives me over the edge with need. I need him inside me, but what would he think of a woman he just met trying to fuck him in a storage room?

His hands continue on their path downward, toying with the hem of my dress a bit before hiking it up over my thick thighs and resting it on my hips. He presses one hand against the front of my panties, and a desperate squeak escapes me, my entire body pulsing at his touch. His fingers tease me as he rubs me through the thin fabric.

"Please," I whisper against his mouth, my lips trembling.

"Please?"

"Please ... touch me," I tell him.

He hooks the side of my panties with a finger and moves them aside, then slips his finger into my opening. I cry out at how good it feels. His palm presses against my clit and pushes the finger in deeper, my walls clasping down around him.

"You're very wet, Bailey," he says, his voice hardly more than a growl in my ear.

"Yes," I say, hardly able to form words. "Yes."

He slips his finger out, and I sigh at the unwelcome emptiness. He grabs my panties in both hands and rolls them down until they're around my ankles, crouching down so I can gingerly step out of them. Then he shoves them in his jacket pocket and stands back up, facing me with those gray eyes.

"You're so beautiful," he says, and I giggle.

"Yeah?"

"Yeah," he says, "you are." One of his hands grabs my bum and squeezes, pulling me forward until his groin is pressing against my stomach. "Can you feel that?" I can feel how rock-hard his cock is through his pants, and I want nothing more than to take it out and have him.

As if he's read my mind, he unzips his pants and undoes his belt. He lets them hang open as he tugs his underwear down just enough for his cock to spring free, the size and thickness of it makes me all the wetter.

He grabs my hips and pulls me forward, my dress still hiked up and leaving me completely exposed. My heels make me the perfect height for my pussy to rub along his bare cock, his hands using my hips to guide me up and down his length.

But he doesn't go inside.

His shaft is glistening with my juices, and all I want is to feel him pressing his way deep inside me. "Please," I ask again, but he shakes his head.

"I don't want our first time to be in here," he says.

"First?" I ask, but the question is quickly forgotten when he kisses me. His hand returns to my groin, this time two fingers pressing past my lips and filling me. "Ohhh," I moan as his fingers work magic. "Oh, fuck."

"I won't fuck you in here," he says, "but I will make you come for me."

His words open the floodgates as I buck my hips forward and bury his fingers inside me. I grind my clit against his palm as he stretches me, and it takes about seven seconds for my body to begin to shake with an overwhelming climax.

"Oh god, I'm coming! I'm coming, Knox!"

"Good," he says, "come for me."

When I finally stop convulsing and am trying to catch my breath, he takes his fingers out of me and pops them in his mouth. He licks them clean, then kisses me hard. It's something Zach would have never done, but it's so, so hot and makes me want to do more with Knox.

A lot more.

———

"There you are!" Cassie cries. "Where were you hiding?" She looks between Knox and me and cocks her head. "Never mind. Come on, the after party is starting in my room upstairs! You have to come open the first bottle of champagne with me!"

I give Knox an apologetic wave. "Guess I have to go. Sorry."

"That's okay," he says. "Go have fun. I'm sure I'll see you around."

Somehow, I believe it.

SEVENTEEN

KNOX

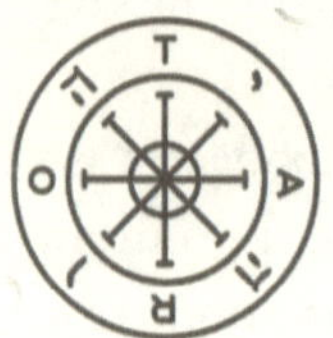

I hang around the hotel for several more hours, waiting until I see Bailey passing through the lobby. I don't let her know I'm there, but I wanted to make sure she left here and got home alright. She piles into an Uber with a couple of other people, and I take off on foot, determined to beat her to her place.

I run on two feet and beat the car, albeit only by a few minutes. Bailey seems to have been the last one dropped off, seeing as she lives in the middle of nowhere. She says something to the driver before climbing out of the car, and the driver hops out to give her the purse she forgot.

"Thanks," she groans, hardly able to stand as she fights to get the purse strap to stay on her wobbling shoulder. She waves to the driver as they turn and head down the long gravel road, then turns and stumbles as she makes her way up onto the deck.

I stay off in the shadows of the trees, watching her but keeping a safe distance. She's never seen me as a man out here, but I'm not much use to her in my wolf form. If she were to trip and hit her head, for example, I'd be much more practical like this. Still, I've no clue how she'd react to seeing me. She might think I'm some stalker.

She digs around in her purse for several minutes before

finding her keys, then fights a while longer to get them into the lock and the door open. She flicks on a light and heads inside, not even bothering to close the door behind her.

"What the ... This girl," I mutter, laughing as I shake my head.

I creep to the door and listen, the house eerily silent. I push the door open slightly with my breath held, and I see her across the open living space. She's passed out on the couch, shoes still on, purse and keys thrown careless on the floor beside her. Her head is tipped back and half hanging off the couch. She's sure to have a lot of neck pain if she spends the entire night lying like that.

I take my shoes off and take slow, silent steps inside. Despite the smell of alcohol that wafts from her, I can still pick up her scent. She smells so good it's dizzying, but right now, I need to focus on taking care of her and getting her safely to bed.

I take her shoes off and put them by the door. I pick up her purse and keys and place them on the island counter where she usually leaves them. Then I scoop her into my arms, cradling her against my chest. She moans something soft and incoherent into the fabric of my dress shirt, my suit jacket now unbuttoned and hanging open.

"Knox was ... Cassie got it ... She ... She got it," she groans, and I can't help but smile at the nonsensical banter.

"Come on, sweetheart," I whisper, carrying her carefully to her bedroom. I set her down on top of the bed. She immediately sprawls out, making it a bit trickier to pull the duvet down from under her so I can properly tuck her in. Once I wrestle it from beneath her, I bring it up over her. I watch her snatch the edge of it and yank it up over her shoulders, snuggling the blanket tightly around her neck.

"Knox, you ... Don't go," she moans, the words generating a bit more sting than I'd have imagined them to.

I sit on the edge of the bed and stroke her hair, laughing when her soft breathing turns into gentle snores. She looks so peaceful as she sleeps, eyelashes fluttering occasionally. I can see her drifting farther away, her breathing slowing as she lands a little deeper in the dreamscape with each passing minute.

And usually, I'd be looking forward to meeting her there.

But now, having had her in person, meeting up in the dreamscape doesn't have the same appeal. I'd still rather spend the time with her there than not, and it's nice that in our dreams, we can go anywhere we like, but nothing compares to the actual feel of her skin on mine, the actual taste of her lips, and the actual warmth of her body pressed against my own.

My thoughts cycle back to how her body was so receptive to me in the closet earlier today. The way she got so wet so quickly at my touch makes me hungry for more. I could feel how badly she wanted me. I wanted her too, but not there, not like that.

I want her here, in a proper bed. I want to make love to her as the sun goes down and wake up and make love to her again as it rises. I want to feel her legs wrap around my hips as I press down into her, her heels digging into me as she pulls me in deeper. I want to leave a trail of kisses from her ankles up to her temples and back down again, stopping at every sensitive spot.

I want her in all the ways; I know I must be patient.

I stroke her hair a few more times before gently kissing her forehead. "Sleep tight, sweetheart," I whisper. She smiles, pulling the blanket in a little tighter. I head out and shut off the lights, closing the front door behind me. The cool night air hits me with the smell of the forest, and I inhale deeply.

I head into the trees and shift, all of my fancy clothes landing in a shredded mess.

Then I go to my usual spot on the deck and curl up, ready for sleep to take me to the dreamscape.

And ready to meet the love of my life there.

Eighteen

Bailey

The sunlight pouring into my window carries the sharp pain of a thousand daggers.

I struggle to open my eyes as the sun's glare hits my face. The birds chirping outside sound like screaming in my ears, and the world feels like it's spinning and ringing. Sitting up makes me feel like I might be sick. I take a few minutes for my stomach to settle before standing. I brace myself on the bedside table, fighting to catch my balance.

"Ugh, god," I sigh, finally wholly upright.

I head into the bathroom and splash some cold water on my face. My hair is a tangled, sweaty ball atop my head. Yesterday's mascara forms raccoon-like rings around both my bloodshot eyes. I look like death and feel worse, but I guess I shouldn't expect any less for how many shots Cassie conned me into taking at that after-party.

I head into the kitchen and gather some Tylenol and a glass of cold water. Then I stagger to the living room and settle down on the couch, pushing the pills past dry lips as I shakily tilt the water to my mouth and down half the glass. I set it down on the coffee table and sigh, falling back against the couch and letting my pounding head fall back. I take in some steadying breaths, willing the world to stop spinning.

Then, a soft sound has me opening my eyes.

The distant sound of scratching grabs my attention. I wait for it to happen again and realize it's coming from the other side of my patio doors. I stand on shaky legs, walk across the room, and pull back the door's curtains. I see a familiar face.

I slide the door open. "Hey, boy!" I say, bending down to pet Wolfie's head. "Were you here last night? I don't remember seeing you." He whines loudly and sits in the doorway as he usually does. Feeling awful, I think some wolf cuddles might be the cure.

"Come on," I tell him, and he excitedly follows me inside as I close the door. We head over to the couch, and I flop down. Wolfie sits on the floor, looking up at me with big, pleading eyes. "Oh, come on," I say, patting the couch beside me. "Get up here."

He jumps up and curls up beside me. He rests his head in my lap and sighs, seeming content.

I look around the room and notice my shoes by the door, my purse, and keys on the island. "That's so funny ... I don't remember putting my stuff away when I got home. I don't remember ... Well, I don't remember much of anything, really. Did you see me come home, Wolfie? Did I put all my stuff away? Geez, drunk me must have her shit more together than regular me. That's sad."

Wolfie whines but doesn't move. I scratch the spot behind his ear that he loves as I reach for the remote. "Wanna watch some TV?" I ask him, waiting as though he might answer. But, of course, he doesn't. He's just a wolf.

I flick on the TV and dig through the newest titles on my streaming app before settling on a cooking show. I don't have the brainpower for anything serious today.

"Guess what, Wolfie? Remember how I said I was hoping to meet someone at the wedding? I did! I did meet someone."

His ears perk up, but he doesn't move. I keep petting him as I gush about how hot Knox was and how attentive and gentlemanly he was while we danced.

"I like him," I say, "but I don't know if I'll ever see him again. I don't even know why he was at that wedding. I don't think he was on the guest list. Maybe he was staying in the hotel and saw me and just wanted to have some fun. Maybe he's a professional party-crasher. Who knows? Although, if he *was* staying at that hotel, it'd be kinda weird to take me to a storage closet instead of his room, right?"

Wolfie cocks his head up and gives me a side-eyed glance.

"Sorry, boy. TMI," I tell him. "I just really, really want to see him again. Honestly, I haven't stopped thinking about him since last night. But that's wild. You can't be obsessed with someone you just met and literally spent a couple hours with. Can you?"

Wolfie whines loudly, nuzzling my cheek with his nose.

"Okay, well, I'm happy you don't think it's weird. The funny thing is ... I swear I know him from somewhere, but I can't place it. But those eyes ... He had these light gray eyes, like yours. Except I've never seen eyes like that on a human before. I've never seen anyone that looked like him before. He looked ... He was beautiful, Wolfie. Just gorgeous. I think you'd approve."

Wolfie howls, and I laugh as I squeeze my temples. "Not so loud, boy! I still have a killer headache."

He whimpers and nuzzles his nose into my neck before laying back down, his head in my lap.

We sit together for hours while I watch cooking shows, and Wolfie sleeps. The TV is on, and it's a peaceful, lazy day, but my brain isn't here. It's back on the dance floor with Knox. It's remembering the way his hand felt pressed against my lower back. It's reminiscing on the way his lips felt against mine, the way his cock felt against ... me.

I sigh. I can't stop thinking about him, no matter how hard I try. I'm unsure how I'll find him, but there must be a way. I grab my phone and search for a couple of social media sites. Knox isn't a common name, but I still come up blank. Maybe I can return to the hotel when I'm feeling better tomorrow and ask the front desk staff if anyone knows him. Surely, I can track him down with a bit of detective work.

There has to be a way to find him because I *have* to see him again.

Nineteen

Knox

"Hey, boy!" she says, bending down and patting my head. "Were you here last night? I don't remember seeing you."

I whine in response, wishing I could shift here and now and tell her everything. She's looking a little worse for wear today, but she's still stunningly beautiful in my eyes. Nothing could make her look any less perfect to me, not even being exceptionally hungover.

"Come on," she says, and I almost lose my shit with how excited I am. Bailey's never invited me into her place while in wolf form. Well, technically she's never invited me into her place whatsoever. But she needed me last night. And I'm not a vampire; I don't have to wait until I'm invited to enter a home. I couldn't leave her asleep on the couch with her neck kinked the way it was. She would have been in even worse shape today if I had.

Putting her to bed and caring for her was the proper thing and what any loving mate would do.

I follow her inside. She shuts the door behind us and heads to the couch, flopping down. I sit on the floor and stare at her, silently begging to join.

"Oh, come on," she says, patting the couch beside her. "Get up here."

She needn't ask me twice as I fly onto the couch and settle in beside her. I rest my head in her lap, sighing contentedly.

"That's so funny," she says, "I don't remember putting my stuff away when I got home. I don't remember ... Well, I don't remember much of anything, really. Did you see me come home, Wolfie? Did I put all my stuff away? Geez, drunk me must have her shit more together than regular me. That's sad."

I whine but don't move. She's scratching the spot behind my ear that I love. It's the only good part about being in wolf form around here. I can tell she's an animal lover, and I'll take her care and affection any way I can, even if I'd rather it be in my human form.

"Wanna watch some TV?" she asks, leaning in for the remote and flicking the television on.

I lay there as she scratches me, my mind constantly wandering back to the thought of the way she felt in my arms. Dancing with her at the wedding was magical, but what happened in the storage closet ... Fuuuck.

I decide to tell her the truth and show her who I am. We're never going to be able to truly be together if I don't show her both sides of me, including the fact that I'm a shifter.

———

I don't know how many hours pass with the two of us curled up on the couch, but I must have dozed off because I open my eyes and realize it's grown dark outside. Bailey stretches and yawns, sitting more upright and patting my back.

"You want to come sleep in my bed with me?" she asks, and now I'm even more sad I'm not in human form.

I whine happily, jumping to follow her as she turns the TV off and heads to her room. I jump up on the bed and stretch out beside her, happy when she throws one of her arms over me. As we lay there and I hear her falling asleep, her rhythmic breaths slowing, I decide tomorrow will be the day.

Tomorrow, I will show Bailey who I am.

———

I'm buzzing in anticipation as I hear her car pulling down the gravel road. Bailey returned to work this morning, but little does she know this is no typical Monday. I've been waiting all day for her to come home so I can show her the truth, and the time is just about here.

She flies out of her car and slams the door, eyes filled with tears. She shakily unlocks the door, not even bothering to say hi. When she opens it, she heads inside but leaves the patio doors wide open.

I follow her cautiously, not wanting to upset her further. I find her facedown on her bed, head stuffed into a pillow as she cries inconsolably. I jump up on the bed, nuzzling my nose into her hair.

"My job sucks, Wolfie!" she cries, words muffled by the pillow. "My boss is such a prick. He threatened to fire me for honoring a coupon that expired yesterday. *Yesterday*, Wolfie! Who fires someone for that? Besides, the lady was 80-something years old. She didn't even know the coupon expired!"

She rolls over, tears streaming down her cheeks from puffy eyes. I stretch out beside her, setting my face beside hers as she continues to vent.

"I don't want to work at the grocer anymore. It sucks! I wanna be a writer."

My ears perk up at the confession. I've seen her sitting on her laptop and typing, but I always assumed she was on social media or chat forums. I didn't realize she might be writing with a purpose.

But I think it's fantastic.

She strokes my fur, the tears on her cheeks drying as we

silently lay there. I decide tonight isn't the best time to show her my transformation. She's isn't in the best headspace. I'll have to pick another night to show her my proper form.

"Thanks for listening to me, Wolfie." I lick her cheek, and she giggles. Her skin is salty and sweet. "I don't know why you decided to show up here one day and never leave … but I'm glad you did. I've been a lot less lonely with you around."

She rolls onto her side and drapes an arm over me. It isn't long before her breathing slows, and I can tell she's fallen asleep. I decide to stay with her tonight. She could use comfort, and I could use her presence.

I drift off to sleep, ignoring the anxious bit of my brain begging to sleep beside her in my human form.

For now, showing her that side again will have to wait.

Twenty

Bailey

Bits of light filter in the kitchen window as I finish the dishes. It's been a few nights since I told Wolfie how I want to be a writer. It's strange; it's not as though confessing this to a wolf should have had any impact on me. But somehow, it has. It's like a weight has been lifted since I said it out loud, and I actually sat down and wrote several hundred words of a short story today.

Funny thing is, it's a short story about a woman who gets lost in the woods and is rescued by a werewolf.

It sounds too cliche to say it came to me in a dream, but it did. Last night, I dreamt I was running through the woods, alone and scared, when a wolf popped out from behind a tree. It shifted into a beautiful man. He looked familiar, but night had fallen, making it hard to make out his features. Still, I somehow knew he was there to protect me.

I'm about done drying the dishes when a sound outside startles me. I freeze, my heart racing in my chest. I never get visitors way out here. My place is hard to find unless you're specifically looking for it, and that's how I like it.

But that sound ... that sound was someone stepping onto the deck, I'm sure of it.

I creep over to the kitchen window and look out, but the sun is setting, and it's pretty dark outside. Then, a loud bang on my glass door makes me jump nearly out of my skin. I stand there, frozen, unsure whether I should answer. I'm not expecting anyone. Maybe someone got lost and ended up down this road and is looking for directions or to borrow a phone.

Another loud bang on the door, followed by a man's voice. "Bee? Bee, I know you're in there. Can you open the door, please?"

Fuck, it's Zach. What the hell is he even doing here? I thought I made it abundantly clear at Cassie's wedding that I wanted nothing to do with him. Wasn't refusing to dance with him enough? Was my dancing with Knox not a clear indication that I'd moved on?

I peek out the kitchen window again, and Zach steps back from the door, our eyes locking.

Fuck, fuck, fuck. Shit. Now he knows I've seen him. I can't lie and say I was sleeping.

I throw the dish towel I was using over my shoulder and take a deep breath. I open the door, my stomach turning, when I realize the idiot is holding a massive bouquet of roses and a bottle of wine. "Hey," he says, his too-white smile as fake as the rest of him. He wreaks of cologne, and all I want is to slam the door in his face and lock it.

"What do you want, Zach?" I ask flatly. "Why are you here?"

"Can we talk? You hardly said two words to me at Cass's wedding."

"We've got nothing to talk about," I inform him. "You're wasting your time here."

His face wrinkles in frustration, but he quickly smooths it out again. "Can I at least come in and set these down? I drove all the way out here." I'm about to protest when he adds, "And I could really use your bathroom."

I sigh angrily. "Fine. You can use the bathroom, but you've got two minutes, and there's nothing for us to talk about."

He nods and steps inside. I shut the patio door as he sets the roses and wine down on the kitchen counter. Then he heads to the bathroom.

I look around but don't see Wolfie anywhere. Last I saw, he was curled up asleep on my bed. I'm sure he'll wake up and come running if I scream. I don't think it'll come to that, but knowing he's here comforts me.

Zach returns and sits on one of the barstools at the kitchen island. "So, we need to talk," he says.

"Uh, no, we sure don't. I just told you that, Zach. There's nothing to talk about."

"Please, Bee, we can—"

"Stop calling me that!" I shout.

"I'm sorry." He sighs. "Look, I know we didn't end on a good note, but—"

"Are you kidding? Is that what you call sleeping with your clients and coworkers? Not ending on a good note?"

"I slept with two people, Bee."

"Does that matter?! You *cheated* on me, Zach. People don't just kiss and make up after stuff like that!"

"Sure they do." He stands up and crosses the room, stopping a couple of feet from where I stand near the door. "Come on, Bee," he coos. "You know I love you, right? I want to make this work."

"There's nothing to make work, Zach! It's over! We're done! Finished! Buh-bye!"

He steps closer, features filling with rage. "You're never going to do better than me, Bailey! I'm successful. I have drive. You work at a grocery store. You were lucky to have a man like me to lean on!"

"I never needed you!" I cry, tears welling up in my eyes. "And I don't want you!"

"I'm not the kind of man who takes 'no' for an answer, Bailey, and I'm not leaving here until you agree to give us another chance!"

Our shouting is interrupted by the sound of growling. We both look to my bedroom doorway, Wolfie's massive stature filling most of the gap as he growls menacingly at Zach.

"Woah," Zach whispers. "Is that a fucking *wolf*?"

"Yeah, and he's my wolf, so you better get out of here!" I tell him.

"Are you fucking *insane*, Bee? You can't keep that thing as a pet! It's a wild animal! It'll eat your face off one night!"

"It's going to eat your face off in a minute if you don't get the fuck out of here," I hiss. "Go."

He glances between Wolfie and I before narrowing his eyes on me. "Fuck. That. You think I'm going to let your new pet scare me out of here? I said I wasn't leaving until you gave me another chance, and I—"

He doesn't finish his sentence before a bright flash fills the room. My eyes take a few seconds to readjust, and when I look again, I see Wolfie's vanished.

And in his place stands a tall, gorgeous man.

Knox.

"What ... What the fuck?" Zach stammers. His eyes are wide with fear as he stumbles backward. He pushes past me and throws the patio door open, screaming into the night as he gets in his car and takes off.

My heart is hammering in my chest. I look back at Knox, but the room starts spinning. Everything goes hazy.

The last thing I remember is the warmth of his body as he pulls me into his arms.

Twenty-One

Bailey

I wake up on my couch, ready to dismiss the entire thing as a crazy dream, when I see him.

Knox.

Knox, the enigmatic man I shared a fleeting connection with at Cassie's wedding, is now perched in my living room chair, engrossed in one of my cherished romance novels. As I begin to stir, he peeks over the book's edge. "Hey," he greets, his deep voice resonating with warmth and familiarity. How are you feeling?"

I sit up, trying to make sense of it all. "Did I ... Did you ... Can you—"

"Yes," he says, seeming to answer everything at once, "but I need to show you. You need to see it with your own eyes, this time without the distraction of your dickhead ex." He sets the book on the coffee table and stands, his nude muscular body delicious in the low light of a corner lamp.

"He *is* a dickhead," I agree, hoisting myself a little more upright. "Okay. Show me."

A flash of light fills the space. I shield my eyes, black dots soiling my vision momentarily. Then I see that Wolfie sits exactly where Knox had been.

"Jesus Christ," I mutter under my breath. "So you ... You really can—"

Wolfie shifts back into Knox, my eyes once again granted the blessing of his full-frontal nudity.

I shield my eyes, unsure why I suddenly feel so shy, considering our encounter at the wedding. "Can you ... I think—"

"I can put something on," he says. "Wait here." He leaves for the bathroom and returns with a towel wrapped around his waist. "Better?"

"Better," I say. "Thanks. It's not that I don't want ... I mean, you look fabulous, it's just that—"

"You don't have to explain yourself to me," he laughs. "I can only imagine how overwhelming this is for you—seeing all this. I'm sorry I didn't tell you sooner. I was just waiting for the right time."

"I see." He sits back in the chair, and I'm quite happy he keeps a bit of distance between us. Despite the wedding and my undeniable pull for him, I don't quite know what to make of this situation. My mind is reeling with everything that's happened. "So, what are you?" I ask.

He nods. "A shifter. I can shift between my wolf and human form at will. Well, usually."

"Is it something you're born with, or—"

"Yes," he says, nodding again. "It comes from a specific gene, more often passed down from the father's side, but it can come from either. It usually manifests during puberty. Everyone in my pack had their shifting abilities by age twelve, except me. I was a bit of a late bloomer, you could say."

"What age were you?"

"Sixteen the first time it happened," he says, "and it was very inopportune. I was about to ... Well, I was with this girl I liked, and—"

"It's okay," I tell him, holding up a hand. "You don't have to explain any more than that."

"Thanks," he says. "Anything else you want to know?"

"I have a million questions, but how come you kept hanging around on my deck as a wolf? Why didn't you initially show me that you were a shifter? And how did you find me all the way out here? Did you stumble upon my cabin one day and think I looked fun?"

He scratches his head. "Bailey, I ... I have something I need to confess to you," he says, those piercing gray eyes chock full of sincerity.

"Okay," I say, "what?"

"You're my fated mate. And ... Well, I used some magic to find you. There's a lady, the Witch of Bonds, people call her, but her name is Agatha."

"Agatha?" I echo. "Why does that sound so familiar?"

"She's a witch," he explains, "and she specializes in pairing mates using a fated tarot deck."

The words hit me like a brick in the chest. "The tarot reader at Cassie's bachelorette party," I say out loud.

"Sure, that's probably how you met her," he says. "I hired her to guide me to my mate, which led me to you. But I lost the ability to shift for a while as a result. I was stuck in my wolf form up until the night of the wedding. That's why I didn't show you the real me sooner. But I still couldn't stay away from you. The pull was too strong. So I stayed and hung around as Wolfie."

"Oh my gosh," I cry, throwing my head into my hands. "I confessed things to wolf-you about human-you! God, that's so embarrassing!"

"I thought it was adorable," he says with a smirk. "Please don't be embarrassed. You couldn't have known."

"No, I couldn't have, but that doesn't make me feel like any less of an idiot," I groan. "And what about the dreams? It was you I kept seeing in all my dreams, wasn't it?"

He nods, grinning sheepishly. "Yeah. Shifter mates can dreamshare, but I had no idea a shifter-human couple could do it!"

"We're not a couple," I correct him, his face immediately flooded with hurt.

"I ... You're my fated mate, Bailey. I know you are. That's why the tarot led me here."

I pinch the space between my brows, and my head suddenly feels like it might explode. "I'm sorry, Knox, but I ... I need time. I just got out of a relationship a couple of months ago, and... I don't think I'm ready to jump right into something else. Plus I need to digest all of this. I'm sorry."

He nods his understanding, head hanging as he sits there in silence. "Okay," he finally says softly, "I understand. I can give you space if that's what you need."

"It is," I assure him. "It really is. I'm sorry, Wolf—I mean, Knox. You have to go."

"I get it," he says. He heads to the kitchen and stands in front of the fridge. I watch as he takes the dry-erase marker and writes something on the magnetic whiteboard I use to scribble notes and grocery lists. "I wrote my number down," he says, replacing the marker. "I hope you understand why, even though I couldn't tell you sooner, I really, really wanted to. And that time at the hotel—"

"Let's not talk about it," I say.

"Fair enough," he says. He takes the towel off, and I avert my eyes as he folds it and sets it on the kitchen island. "I hope you'll text me, Bailey."

"Bye, Knox," I say, and he shifts back into his wolf form and takes off into the night.

TWENTY-TWO

It feels as though my heart is being torn from my very chest as I leave her. I run away from her cabin, her scent dissipating far too quickly as I struggle to breathe without her near. I don't want to leave her. Everything in me is screaming to stay and explain to her why we need to be together.

But a bigger part of me is scared, terrified to push too hard and push her away.

I run through the night, my legs burning from exertion. It's nearly dawn by the time I make it back to my place, and I shift into human form to take a hot shower and put some fresh clothes on.

My clothes.

It's been far too long since I wore my own things or slept in my own bed. But that's how much she means to me. I'd rather her than all my usual niceties. I'd sacrifice everything if it meant getting her to see that we're meant to be together.

Hopefully she can see that on her own, sooner than later.

I head back to the camp where my pack resides, a bunch of loud hoots and hollers breaking out at my arrival.

"Where the hell have you been hiding?" Drew, one of my packmates, asks.

"Been busy," I say. "You know, working and stuff."

He shoots me a disbelieving stare. "Really? Because I went around your place and you weren't there. I went there a couple times."

"I took a little trip for a couple days," I shrug. "Was feeling a bit overworked. Needed to cut loose."

"Cut loose, hey?" he says with a cheeky grin. "Uh huh."

"Never you mind," I groan. "How have things been around here?"

———

Days pass. Everyone is glad to have me back, which is nice, but all the company in the world can't make up for her absence. Life without her feels empty and heavy, and all I want is to be curled up in her bed, sleeping beside her once more.

Even if it's with four legs and her calling me 'Wolfie'.

I sand the side of the cabinet I'm working on, making sure every inch is smooth before I stain it. Then, a chiming sound comes from my pocket. I pull out my phone, my face lighting up when I see the message.

> I'm not ready to dive into anything. I just got out of a bad relationship. Can we get to know each other?

My heart pounds as I think about what to say back.

> I'd like that.

———

Over the next few weeks, Bailey and I text each other night and day. It's not the same as having her in person, but I can tell she's slowly growing to trust me, which warms my heart.

———

Good morning handsome. You up?

> Ish. And good morning, gorgeous. You busy
> today?

Ya. Work. You know how it is.

> I do.

You busy making cabinets?

> Yeah. Got a big order that needs to be done
> by Friday.

Need a hand?

> You serious? What do you know about
> cabinets?

Literally: nothing lol

> Lol

———

> Hey pretty lady

Hey handsome. What's up?

> Nothing. Just thinking bout you.

Oh yeah? What about me?

> Just how I wish we were watching cooking
> shows together.

Ha, yeah right. You even like that stuff?

> I do! I love food!

Haha, I believe it. Well. Maybe someday.

———

Hey. You up?

Barely. What's up?

I can't sleep. Thought I'd bug you if you were still up. But I'll let you sleep.

No way! I'm up now, lol

Lol, k. I kinda miss sleeping beside you, FYI

Even if you are really hairy

Hey! It's not hair. It's fur

And it keeps me warm

It keeps me warm too! That's why I miss it

Oh that's why? Just that?

Maybe

Maybe? Why else

Maybe I just miss you

I miss you too

———

Hey

Hey

What's up

Nothing. You free today?

If not all good

No I'm free. What's up?

Was wondering if you wanted to get coffee

I realized the other day that we've fooled
around in a closet but we've never had a
proper date lol

Lol you are not wrong

I would love to take you for coffee

Hey I'm the one who asked you! It's me taking
you for coffee lol

Oka okay! You're a strong independent lady, I
get it lol

That's right. I am.

You are,

Wanna say tomorrow at 11? There's a cafe
across the street from my work, we can go
before my shift

It's a date

:) <3

————

Thank you for coffee

My pleasure

Hey Bailey?

Yeah?

Can I kiss you next time?

Yes please.

Can next time be tomorrow? ;)

Haha sorry handsome, I work a double tomorrow! This weekend?

Deal :)

———

I really like kissing your face

I really like kissing yours too

But

Wouldn't mind kissing other parts of you either. Just FYI

I think that can be arranged sometime ;)

YAY

Lol

So you were saying at coffee you own your own land?

Ya. I have a cabin, kinda like yours. Not gonna lie, yours is way nicer lol

Lol that's okay I don't own mine. And where does your pack live?

They have a camp nearby. Kinda like a little town

Cute

It's nice. You'd like it.

Maybe ill have to see it one day

I'd like that :)

TWENTY-THREE

BAILEY

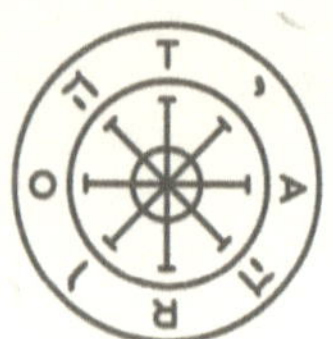

My phone lights up, and I smile as I see Knox's messages. The screen is obnoxiously bright to my still-adjusting eyes, but it's the first thing I want to check when I wake up each morning.

> Good morning gorgeous

> Missing you

We've gotten into a ritual of texting each other 'Good morning' and 'Good night' every single day, me always calling him handsome and me beautiful. These past few weeks getting to know each other have been magical, and it starts to sink in just how deeply I'm falling in love with him.

How deeply I've *fallen* in love with him.

And the pull between us, the one he's been saying he could feel all along, has only been getting stronger each day.

I realize that I need to give in to whatever this is. I trust Knox completely. He's been a gentleman and more than patient with me. I need him to know I feel the same, even if the thought terrifies me.

Good morning handsome

Busy today?

It's a bit of work, but not much. Would love to
see you

I'd love to see you too. Can I come over
someday soon?

What about Saturday?

Yeah, Saturday works.

Sweet :)

It's a date

———

Saturday comes. I head to Knox's house, my heart caught in my throat the entire drive. I've memorized the way to his place from mine. The winding backroads get me there in record time. He's raking leaves out front when I get there, his face lighting up when he sees me.

"Hey," he says, taking my hands in his mine after I shut my car door. "How was the drive?" He pecks my lips, and I immediately want him to kiss me a thousand more times.

"It was good," I say. "Coffee?"

"Sure, let's go inside." He takes my hand and leads me into his place. I love how it smells; scents of pine and freshly cut wood fill the air. The smell of coffee soon joins them as Knox brews us a pot and pours me a cup.

"Here you go," he says, handing me a mug as we settle on his couch.

"Thanks," I say, letting the mug warm my hands. "Hey, there's a reason I wanted to come over today."

"Oh?" he says, slurping his coffee as he stares at me over his mug. "Other than that, I'm awesome, and you missed me?"

I laugh. "I mean, facts, but those aren't the only reasons."

"Alright," he says, looking curious. "What's up?"

I set my coffee down and scoot closer to him on the couch. He sets his mug down, his gray eyes mesmerizing as I sit there and stare at him. "I ... I needed to tell you something."

He takes my hands in his and squeezes, his hands warming me more than the coffee. "You know you can always tell me anything, Bailey."

I smile. "I know. I ... I want you to know that I think I've fallen in love with you, Knox Roffe."

He stares at me a moment, eyes fixed on mine. The anticipation of what he might say kills me, but he doesn't answer. Instead he leans forward, planting the softest of kisses on my lips. "I love you too, Bailey Dennis," he replies, his lips hovering above mine.

I press my mouth against his hard. The way he says my name sends a million shivers down my spine. I let him linger against my lips a while before shoving my hands up into his hair, pulling him harder into the kiss and eliciting a guttural moan from him.

"Can I be your mate?" I ask breathily.

"I thought you'd never ask," he jokes, "but there's one problem with that."

I look at him, eyes wide. "Oh? And what's that?"

"You already *are* my mate."

I squeal with delight as his strong hands slide under my legs and cup my buttocks. He picks me up as though I'm weightless, my legs instinctively wrapping around his waist as he carries me off to his bedroom.

He lays me down on the bed, the soft blankets cradling me as he wrestles with the top button of my pants. He stands at the end of the bed as he unzips them and rolls them down my legs, carefully pulling them past my feet and neatly folding them before setting them on his dresser.

His mouth is fire against my thighs, his lips trailing hot kisses up each one as I squirm with need. He hoists my shirt up and kisses my belly and down my mound, my hips elevating off the bed as my body begs for more. He gives me what I need, his mouth finding my sweet spot as he begins licking and sucking. I cry out as his tongue swirls in circles around it, each movement driving me a little closer to the edge.

"Please," I whimper, "I need you, Knox. I need you ... inside."

His pants are off before I open my eyes. He flips his shirt over his head, the rest of his clothing tossed messily around the room. I look down at his cock, having forgotten how big it was since fooling around at Cassie's wedding.

He kneels above me on the bed, lowering himself down until I feel the tip of his thick cock teasing and poking at my entrance. My breath ceases as I feel him beginning to part me, his hips moving slowly with care.

He kisses the corner of my mouth as I gasp. "You okay?" he asks.

I nod. "I'm okay. Just go slow."

"I will," he says. He kisses along my cheek and down my jawline, eventually kissing along the side of my neck. He feels terrific as he presses his way inside me, the length of him pushing in deeper and deeper as he fills and stretches me.

His mouth finds mine, and he nibbles on my bottom lip, causing me to whimper. I press my hips upward, urging more of him inside. He doesn't move very fast, but the long, rhythmic strokes of his hips and the way his pelvis presses against my clit both send me over the edge.

"Oh, Knox, I'm gonna—"

"Me too," he groans. "Fuck, Bailey, I'm coming."

"Me too," I cry. "come in me, please, Knox."

I feel him filling me as my orgasm fires up my every nerve-ending. I scream his name and dig my fingers into his shoulders, realizing I never want to go another day without this.

I never want to go another day without him by my side.

Epilogue

Knox

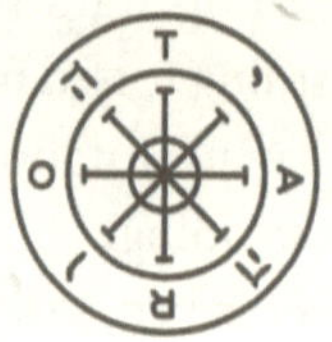

A FEW MONTHS LATER

Her brows make the squiggly shape I recognize as her concentration face. I smile, knowing she's thinking hard about what to write next.

"How's the project going, Bay?" I ask, my voice laced with a hint of intrigue.

"Good, good," she says, her eyes fixed on the laptop screen, her fingers dancing on the keyboard. "I'm torn between making it their parents who oppose their love. What's your take on this?"

"Why not both?" I ask.

She looks up with a beaming smile. "Perfect," she nods, fingers clacking away at the keyboard.

"Hey, why don't you take a break?" I suggest, the aroma of the ground turkey wraps wafting through the room. "I made some lunch. Those ground turkey wraps you love so much."

"Mmm, yeah, that sounds good. I just ... wanna ..."

"Bay!" I shout, walking over and playfully tickling her ribs. "Come have food with me!"

She swats my hands away. "Okay, but not if you keep tickling me!" She rubs her protruding belly. "You're not allowed to torture me right now! I'm being tortured enough by our unborn."

"He comes by it honestly," I say with a shrug.

"Or she!" Bailey harps, raising a brow. "It *could* be a girl, you know."

"And that would be fine," I remind her, "but it's not."

"You're so stubborn," she says, standing from her desk. She kisses my cheek before shuffling to the dining area. "Alright, let's eat then."

If anyone had asked me seven months ago if I was ready to be a father, I'm not sure what I'd have said. But I couldn't feel more excited or more prepared than I am now. We've been planning our baby's arrival since day one, and the cabin is already prepared and equipped with a nursery, baby-proofed everything, and a stockpile of clothes, diapers, and other things.

My pack has also been amazingly supportive. People have given us things, bought us things, and helped paint and prep the baby's room. Everyone has welcomed Bailey with open arms and been extremely helpful to her despite the fact that she's a human. I was surprised; our pack had never agreed to let a human live with us before.

Even shifters know there's no fighting it when someone is your destined mate.

A knock on the door has Bailey and I exchanging confused looks. "Were you expecting someone today?" she asks.

I shake my head. "Were you?"

"No," she says.

"Hmm." Whoever it is knocks again, and I head to the door and open it, curious who could have wandered out here and landed at my door. My eyes grow wide as I see her standing there, grinning ear to ear. "Agatha! What are you doing here?"

Bailey comes waddling over, opening the door wider so she can see the witch as well. "Yeah, just what *are* you doing here, Agatha?"

She puts her hands up defensively. "Please, I'm not your

enemy! After all, wasn't me and my magic that helped bring you lovebirds together?"

Bailey sighs. "I guess that's true."

"What do you want?" I ask. "I thought I paid my dues to the tarot."

"You have," she nods, "and the tarot thanks you. I heard the two of you were expecting a child, so I just wanted to drop in and offer you a present for the little tyke. A sort of housewarming gift, I suppose you could say."

Bailey and I glance at each other, then look back at the witch.

Agatha pulls a black velvet bag from somewhere inside her cloak, handing it to me and then offering a polite nod. "I won't take up any more of your time," she says. She turns to leave, calling over her shoulder, "Best of luck to you two!"

I look down at the bag for only a second, but Agatha has vanished when I look up again.

"What do you think it is?" Bailey asks, but I don't dare guess.

"I don't know. Let's go see."

I shut the door and bring the bag to the living room, riddled with curiosity. Bailey and I sit on the couch as I set the bag down on the table, pulling at its drawstrings enough to open the top of it. I reach into the bag, my arm going far deeper than it should for the length of the bag.

I pulled them out one by one: a handmade picture frame made from gnarled twigs, an infant-sized cloak that matches Agatha's, and a tarot card.

The Wheel

Bailey picks up the card, examining either side of it. "This is the card I pulled during the tarot reading!"

I laugh. "That's funny. That's the card I picked when I went to Agatha to get her to help me find my mate."

"Weird," Bailey whispers. "Do you think this is it? The exact card? Wouldn't that mean she doesn't have a full deck anymore?"

I shrug. "Maybe she's got more than one. Maybe she used magic to make a copy of it. Who knows?"

"Good point." Bailey picks up the tiny cloak, running her fingers over the black velvet. "This is kinda cute."

"You're not seriously considering putting our child in that, are you?" I ask.

"Why? You don't like it?"

"I think it's a bit tacky," I tell her. "Besides, I've never seen a shifter wear a cloak."

"Hey, our baby is going to be half-human!"

I laugh. "I've never seen a human wear a cloak like that, Bay."

"Yeah, good point. That picture frame is super cute and rustic, though. We'll have to put our first family photo in there."

"That we will," I agree. I take the picture frame and set it on the fireplace mantle, then I sit back down beside my beautiful mate, kissing her cheek softly. "I love you," I say.

"I love you too," she says. "So very much. You're going to be an amazing father."

"Not half as amazing as you'll be as a mother," I reply.

She kisses me again, her perfect lips lingering on mine. "Come on, let's go to bed early."

"Sounds good to me," I say.

And nothing in the world could sound better.

About the Author

Growing up in a small town in Maine, Mia's childhood was full of countless books filled with love stories, adventure, mystery, and, at times, magic. Her love for these tales grew into a passion for storytelling and filling uncounted notebook pages with vibrant characters.

Through the busyness and stresses of life, Mia always returns to her characters and imagined places, keeping writing as her passion and her outlet to unwind, recharge, and recenter. She currently lives in Maine with her husband and two boys.